Florence Caddy

Household Organization

Florence Caddy

Household Organization

ISBN/EAN: 9783337401474

Printed in Europe, USA, Canada, Australia, Japan

Cover: Foto ©Andreas Hilbeck / pixelio.de

More available books at **www.hansebooks.com**

HOUSEHOLD ORGANIZATION.

BY

MRS. CADDY.

" From my tutor I learnt endurance of labour, and to want little, and
to work with my own hands."—EMPEROR MARCUS AURELIUS.

LONDON :

CHAPMAN AND HALL, 193, PICCADILLY.

1877.

PREFACE.

ONE fine August bank-holiday many thoughts, more or less connected with the day, prompted me to write this essay, so forcibly did it appear that people required help to make their lives easier and happier.

Since then there have been several bank-holi-days; and though trade is depressed throughout the country, though financial panic has ruined thousands, yet the demand for beer, spirits, and tobacco is as great as ever; the hollow gaieties of life are as noisy as ever—perhaps the more so for being more hollow; still our most precious friends kill themselves with overwork—mental pulveriza-tion. If they eased their minds by employing their hands they might yet live, even though many could not, last autumn, afford to buy the breath of sea or mountain air which would have strengthened them for the burdens of the new year. Those who were wise and who had capital invested it in health, that being likely to bring them in the best return.

We have had seven years of the highest national prosperity. Although fictitious, it gave us pleasure while it lasted, and we were able to enjoy all that life has to offer in its perfection. We may be going to pass through seven years of dearth, so we must husband our resources of health and wealth, instead of drawing upon them in the reckless way we have lately accustomed ourselves to do. Some years of scarcity may be a blessing to us all, if they lead us back from the habits of excess and idleness we have fallen into, and particularly the craving for excitement, whether in the form of literature, or by means of stimulants and cordials (absinthe).

A plain but short statement of our national losses will show the necessity of economizing the goods we still possess, financial as well as physical.

Independent of the stagnation of trade which

paralyzes every branch of our commerce, we have lately had losses through foreign loans more severe than any we have experienced during the present century.

Since the announcement by Turkey in October, 1875, that the interest on the Turkish debt would be reduced, there has been a great fall in foreign stocks. The debt of Turkey—roughly speaking, £200,000,000—has fallen, say, £125,000,000 in value. Egyptian securities, not including the floating debt, approximately estimated at £60,000,000, have fallen some £20,000,000 in value. In smaller stocks the fall has probably been some £20,000,000 ; and since the breaking out of the Eastern Question, Russian stocks, at an aggregate of about £165,000,000, have fallen 12 per cent., or a sum equal to more than £20,000,000 sterling.

Besides these calamities there have been in England, as shown by a recent return, 1,797 commercial failures, representing liabilities of £30,000,000 sterling, and it has been calculated that of the firms and persons occupied in business,

3 per cent. have been unable to meet their engage-
ments.

These losses will account for less familiar faces
being seen in the Park in the season, for the
numerous houses unlet in fashionable quarters,
for grouse-moors going almost begging; and,
among many other significant facts, Tattersall,
who generally has 150 applications for coachmen
on his books, has now 150 coachmen applying
to him for situations.

In our present abundance of money, through
dearth of safe investments, many persons have
purchased art treasures; which would be wise,
but for the pain it always causes to part with
things that have once adorned our homes, which
makes this not a happy speculation.

It would be the part of a screech-owl to cry
Woe! woe! and hoot triumphantly over the distresses of our country; but there seems so much
of hope and promise in the fact of our meeting
reverses of fortune with courage, that we cannot
feel that a real disaster has overtaken us. We
have in the case of France an example of how

a great nation can rise renewed in strength out of overwhelming troubles, and our trial is less severe than that of France.

It is not good for any people to sit down to eat and drink and rise up to play, any more than it is good for children to feed upon delicacies in lieu of simple fare. Persons suddenly reduced from affluence to comparative poverty may be glad of a few hints to show them how happiness and refinement are by no means incompatible with a smaller condition of fortune, with a shorter purse; for, after all, the purse is not the pleasure, it only helps us to procure it; our own taste and feeling must teach us what true pleasure is.

It may be demurred that some of the household improvements suggested in this book would be expensive to carry out—such, for instance, as the arrangement of the kitchen; and this is true : but looked at as an investment, they would yield large interest, and it might be prudent to invest under one's own eye, in one's own house, some of the capital we cannot afford to sink. If used in economizing wages, it will give us a profitable return.

We do not hesitate to lay out money in improvements on our farms. Why, then, need we fear to arrange our dwellings in accordance with principles of true economy, so that the ladies of our families may be able to co-operate with us in advancing the benefit of all? Every family might be its own Economical Housekeeping Company (Limited), comprising in itself its shareholders and board of directors, realizing cent. per cent. for its money, because £200 a year would go as far as £400.

If we save the money we now spend upon keeping servants to do our work for us, we shall have more to spend on our holidays, and so shall feel all the more refreshed by our respite from work.

Much is said in this book about superfluities, but although some passages may seem to give colour to such an idea, it is by no means wished to convey the recommendation that our homes and lives are to be bare of beauty. On the contrary, I hanker after profusion and love plenty, but wish them to be placed where they will not give more labour than pleasure, where they will not hamper our every movement at every moment, making us ever wear a sort of moral tight kid-gloves, be the weather hot or cold.

The rock which theories split upon is that they generally presuppose that we can make our lives, and are in independent position and good circumstances, whereas this is seldom the case. The majority of us are neither in good circumstances nor independent: often we have had no control over the purchase of our very furniture; so we must make the best of what we have, only, when we have the opportunity of making a change, let it be a reform as well as a change. My main object in writing this essay has been to show how frequently, and in how short a time, the saving effected by a reform covers the cost of carrying it out.

In the case of young couples about to marry, and beginning to plan their lives, any work will be good which aids them to lay down their plans according to rules of economy and common sense.

January, 1877.

CONTENTS.

THE DIFFICULTY.

THE REMEDY.

THE ENTRANCE-HALL.

BREAKFAST.

THE KITCHEN.

THE LADY-HELP.

THE DINING-ROOM.

THE DRAWING-ROOM.

BED AND DRESSING ROOMS.

THE EDUCATION OF GIRLS.

SUNDAY.

HOUSEHOLD ORGANIZATION.

THE DIFFICULTY.

Impossibility of getting good servants—Over-civilization—Labour has been made hideous—Sleeping partnership—Wealth exempt from this difficulty—Refinement of the professional class—Credit —Phase of insecurity and scarcity—Sweet are the uses of adversity—English people do not fear work—Servants too readily changed—Wilfulness of servants—Upper servants are easily obtained—Servants feel the pressure of the times—Ornamental servants costly luxuries—Two questions—Work must be efficiently done—Woman's work—Misuse of time—We keep servants to wait upon each other—Idleness—Pleasure made a toil.

FOR a long time past we, the middle-classes of England, have felt a great household perplexity, one which has been a daily burden to us all. This is the difficulty, almost impossibility, of getting good servants.

B

Machinery, though it has lightened other branches of labour and cheapened production, has not helped us much here. Social science has been deeply studied, but nothing practical has yet been brought to bear upon this vexed question. The theories are good, the projected reforms better ; but so far there is nothing that people of average intellect, and moderate income, can take hold of and apply to their own case. During the late plethora of wealth throughout the nation, we have so multiplied our wants, and so refined upon the ruder social ideas of the early part of the century, that our servants have not been able to keep pace with our requirements ; and notwithstanding that the lower orders have much more careful education than they had formerly, it seems to be of a sort which makes them discontented with their work, rather than instructing them how to do it better.

In fact, we have degraded labour by making it hideous, by pushing it into holes and corners, by shrinking from it ourselves, and casting it entirely into the hands of the lower orders; until we English are virtually divided into a contemplative and a working class. This would be all very well if it were true that our class could afford to pay liberally for work done well ; but, in effect, the majority of those who wish to be relieved from work cannot pay liberally for hired labour, neither can the bulk of the labouring class perform their part of the bargain in a manner deserving liberal payment.

We have tried to keep ourselves as sleeping partners in the domestic concern ; we have derived profit from our money invested in service, and we find that this is no longer a profitable investment. There is a large wealthy order exempt from these difficulties. By having ample means of recompense, it has the flower of service at its command, and the domestic economy of the mansions of England is perfect. Under steward and housekeeper, this may be compared to the beautiful system seen on board a large ship of war, for discipline, routine, and celerity of service. In both instances the reverse of the shield shows the injurious effects on the lower ranks of a large proportion of unoccupied time, spent in merely waiting for their hours of duty.

The suggestions I have to offer are not required
by this wealthy class—the upper ten thousand, as
they are popularly called, whose incomes range
among the four and five figures; but help seems
to be much needed by the upper twice ten hundred
thousand who have incomes described by three
figures, and who yet, by good birth, breeding, and
education, form the backbone of England; whose
boys, though only home-boarders at Eton, Harrow,
and Rugby, fill all the other large schools of Great
Britain, and whose daughters are the flowers of
our land.

Of late years England has been passing through
a period of unexampled prosperity, so much so as
to make the customs of wealth a familiar habit
with even those who only possess a competence.
To them the domestic difficulty is very great, since
they exact from inferior servants the quality of
service that can only be obtained from the best
trained of their order. This occasions disappointment and irritation. The people whose means are
inadequate to the gratification of their tastes
belong mainly to the professional classes, whose

brain-work most demands repose at home; yet these are, beyond all others, perplexed by the increasing toils and troubles of home life. They find that a struggle which should be peace, and so the whole machinery of their lives is thrown out of gear.

This upper working-class is so occupied by endeavours to make the fortune, or, if not fortune, at any rate to make both ends meet—which has been denied them by birth or accident—that they have no time nor energy left to think these things out for themselves. So they go on bearing the yearly increasing load piled upon them by the tyranny of fashion, of custom, or by their wish to keep up their credit in the eyes of the world; for their credit is in many cases their fortune, and it must be upheld at any sacrifice. A question occurs to many: Is this credit best maintained by out-ward appearances, or is it more firmly secured by seeming strong enough to dispense with artificial support? And, again, Is our money credit the best we can have?

A man of known wealth may go about in a

shabby coat, a countess may wear a cheap bonnet, a Sidonia may dine off bread and cheese. If Gladstone fells trees, he is still Gladstone ; if Ruskin grubs up a wood, he is still a great poet.

Without becoming mere *dilettanti,* may we not enjoy a reputation for taste, and so allow ourselves to be heedless of a few of the conventional proprieties of life ; as a tree rises above the level of the grass ? May we not strive, by the culture of our manners and discourse, to make our simpler social entertainments as highly prized as the feasts of our richer neighbours ? The years of prosperity have passed away, and we seem to have entered upon a phase of society when scarcity and insecurity overwhelm or threaten us all ; when the wealth of yesterday has crumbled into dust, the paper money shrivelled as if it had been burnt. We still have the same high culture, the tastes and feelings of yesterday ; and unfortunately, the same habits of Idleness, Helplessness, Waste, and Luxury.

These are hard charges to bring against the cream of a nation which for centuries has held its own by its energy, abundance of resource, strength of character, and scorn of effeminacy; but it is impossible to deny that these characteristics of the British race have been much less strongly marked of late years. Still, these things are in our nature, and we must not weakly let ourselves decline from our former high standard.

Let us, at the outset of our adversity, meet our altered circumstances with the strength of mind and wisdom befitting English people. Although wealth may be taken from us, we have our education and energy left, which, if properly used, will not allow us to sink into a lower condition than we have hitherto enjoyed; and while we hold our ground we shall strengthen our health, develop our ability, and increase our happiness.

Let us, the women of England, encourage and support the men in an endeavour to return to simplicity of life, to a more manly condition; call it Spartan, Roman, republican, what you will, it is, in fact, the training of soul and body. We have had a long holiday; let us return to school with renewed vigour. We women have been much to blame for the degeneracy which has been felt of late. If men trifle away their time and health upon tobacco, women are foolishly helpless, and they permit their dependants to be wantonly wasteful. Both men and women pass the best hours of daylight in their beds, and make their meals the important event of their days.

Englishmen abroad do not mind work—indeed, they may be said to love it—and never since the days of Drake have they felt it to be a degradation. He said " he would like to see the gentleman that would not set his hand to a rope and hale and draw with the mariners ; " and herein the English differ from continental nations. But in England they let their love of bodily exertion have its scope almost exclusively in their games. Nor do Englishwomen in the Colonies shrink from work, and they are never in the least ashamed of it. You hear them talk quite freely of how Colonel So-and-so called in the morning while they were " stuffing the veal," to ask for the two first dances at the ball at Government House in the evening.

It seems to be only in England that we dread to be seen doing anything useful. And unless we soon cast off this fear we shall be condemned to the deadly-liveliness of Hotel Companies (Limited), with their uninteresting routine; for the supply of servants not being forthcoming at our price, we must of necessity be reduced to this levelling American system, which will flatten all individuality out of us.

One cause of the ever-increasing difficulty of holding a staff of servants well in hand is that our connection with them is too easily changed or dissolved at pleasure. We should bear ourselves very differently towards each other if we knew we were compelled to live together during even one year certain. As the case now is, we do not get to know each other, and a small trial of temper on either side is the prelude to a change. The old patriarchal feeling of considering the servants as members of the family has quite died out, and so their relation to us has become confused. At times we rate them with the tradespeople who come periodically to polish our bright stoves, clean our chandeliers, and wind our clocks, and so we only care whether they do their specified work well or ill, taking no further trouble about them ; sometimes we treat them as the horses which draw our carriage, and see that they are well fed accordingly; and sometimes we look upon them as machines merely.

We hear it said, servants do not take the interest in their places that they used to do ; they are ready to leave you on the smallest provocation ; they will not be told how to do any particular thing ; they have their way, and if you do not like it, well, they think your place will not suit them.   Indeed, one of the most docile and obliging among the servants I have known, on differing with his employer about some work in which he was engaged, said, " Well, I'll do it a little bit your way, and a little bit my way ; and that will be fair, won't it, mum ? "

It is easy enough to get servants of the superior grades—ladies'-maids, parlour-maids, and even house-maids, where two footmen are kept; but is there such a being as a really good plain cook, or has a servant-of-all-work been heard of lately? Although it is truly said that servants themselves are beginning to feel the pressure of the times, this is not from their actual losses by money-market panics, but from the fact that many domestics are out of place on account of those families who have met with losses dispensing with unnecessary assistance. But that does not ease our case, for we are none the less helpless and dependent. Although many upper servants are out of place, this does not make them seek our situations; and if they did so, they would do us a positive injury by bringing into our houses the habits of wealthier families. The reduction of wages, and lack of suitable situations in England, will cause these unemployed servants to seek in emigration the high wages they are still secure of in the Colonies, or in America. There they will be a godsend, and they may reasonably look forward to establishing themselves permanently and happily.

Independently of the collapse of foreign securities and the general depression of trade, the increased cost of all necessaries makes it impossible to many of us to allow ourselves luxuries, of which the most costly are ornamental servants ; and the difficulty of obtaining any others makes it incumbent on us to put our own shoulders to the wheel, and try by diligent self-help to solve some of the problems which so miserably defy us to find a practical answer.

In this consideration of the subject of domestic work in middle-class households, I hope to show in what way the mistress may be rendered more self-reliant, and how the master's purse may be spared the perpetual drain the present system entails upon it at both ends, and from every mesh.

This is but a fraction of a vast subject, yet it is in itself so large, and stretches out into such a variety of kindred topics, that it is difficult to compress it into a form small enough to be easily handled, and still more difficult to make suggestions of reform generally palatable, since many vanities must be hurt by a proposal to reduce establishments, and sensitive feelings wounded by the bluntness of two direct practical questions—

1st. Must the great majority of our young ladies be elegant superfluities?

2nd. Must we keep many servants to wait upon each other?

These questions I hope to answer usefully in the following pages.

We must begin with the understanding that in every house there is work to be done, and that somebody must do it. Our aim will be to reduce its compass, and to do what remains in the cheapest and pleasantest way. But it must be efficiently done, which is seldom the case when young ladies play at housekeeping, which too often means giving out the pepper, and such like. We have long shrunk from allowing our women to work at all. Husbands and fathers have taken a pride in keeping the ladies of their households in that state of ease that no call need be made on them to lift a finger in the way of useful work; so that if reverses befal them, their condition is deplorable indeed.

Now we are turning round and insisting upon every woman being able to support herself by her own exertions. Though a great part of woman's natural work has been taken out of her hands by machinery, this, which is mainly the preparation of clothing, was the occupation of her uncultivated leisure, and did no more than fill up the time which we now devote to culture. By retreating from our active household duties we now divide our time between culture and idleness, or the union of both in novel-reading.

For many years conscientious teachers tried to drive us to household work by calling it our duty : a dull name, sternly forbidding us to find pleasure or interest therein. It was a moral dose of physic, salutary but disagreeable. In the same way we were taught to make shirts and mend stockings, but an evening dress was held to be frivolity. Taste was discouraged, and beauty driven out of our work ; no wonder, then, that the young and careless shunned it altogether, and threw as much of it as they could into the hands of hirelings. Is there no way of teaching duty without making it repulsive by its dreariness and ugliness ?

Now that we pride ourselves upon being no

longer weak-minded and silly, let us exert ourselves to act upon Lord Bacon's maxim, " Choose
the life that is most useful, and habit will make
it the most agreeable." We need not fear that
the routine of daily handiwork—which will become
interesting to us as we try to make it agreeable—
will interfere with our further intellectual culture.
And even should it do so, are not our leaders of
thought beginning to perceive that manual labour
is more commercially valuable than mental labour ;
that the demand for the former is greater as the
supply becomes perceptibly less ? The deadness
of machine work causes us to prize the spirited
and varied touch that can only be imparted by
the hand. Every woman, among her acquaintance,
knows some one who is a skilful, energetic manager
of her house, and yet whose reading and accomplishments are above the average. Indeed, as I
heard one of my friends of this stamp say, when
asked how she found time for so much sketching
from nature, " One always finds time for what one
likes to do."

We see what priceless possessions we lose by our

misuse of time, or waste of it in inanities, when
we look at the embroideries and other work of our
ancestresses, and compare these with the poor
results of our months and years. We see splen-
did embroideries of the time of Titian, with the
needlework still strong enough to outlast all our
nonsense in "leviathan stitch" and "railroad
stitch;" and old lace, by the side of which our
work of mingling woven braids and crochet in
such a manner as to get most show for the least
cost of taste, labour, and invention, is worth
nothing at all.

With regard to my second question—Must we
keep many servants to wait upon each other?—I
will here make one observation.

The heaviest part of the work of a cook and
kitchen-maid consists in preparing the kitchen
meals. Six servants require as many potatoes
peeled, and as many plates, knives, forks, etc.,
cleaned, as six ladies and gentlemen. Mul-
tiply their five meals a day by six, and you will
find that there are thirty plates, knives, forks
spoons, cups or glasses, and many other things,

to be laid on the table, used, washed, and put away again, at a computation of only one plate to each meal.

Think of the time alone consumed in this, and the breakage ; and this merely in the meals.

I am not considering the houses which require a complement of ten servants to keep their machinery in motion, as these do not form part of my subject ; but this slight calculation will enable us to form some estimate of the cost of maintaining a large retinue.

We may well ask why we have drifted into this enormous expenditure, and for what purpose we have gradually let our houses be filled up by a greedy and destructive class, who, notwithstanding many bright exceptions, seem to combine the vices of dirt, disorder, extravagance, disobedience, and insolence. Why, indeed ? For this simple reason, that we are idle. Gloss it over as we may, by calling it a desire to secure time for higher ends, the truth remains the same ; we have neglected our duty in order that we may live in idleness and devote ourselves to pleasure. But if our lives

c

are to be spent in pleasure, we shall ourselves degenerate; for pleasure wears out the body more than work, and excitement more than both. Let us take our appointed burden of steady work, and bear it onwards cheerfully and patiently. By so doing we shall feel it grow gradually lighter. It is not such slavery as the oar to which we chain ourselves. The artificial strain on our lives must be kept up by stimulants, and idleness must be roused by excitement. But our routine of gaiety is no idleness; and as for its name—gaiety—there never was a term more false. The gaiety is a hollow mockery, masking fatigue, untruth, and disappointment.

Sidney Smith says, "One of the greatest pleasures of our lives is conversation." If we will simply allow ourselves to talk upon subjects of common interest, we shall find social gatherings less wearisome than when we have to manufacture small-talk for civility's sake alone. If we meet together for enjoyment instead of for display, we shall replace dissipation—mere dissipation of time (what an endeavour for mortals, whose time is their life!)—by gaiety of heart, which is the best restorative to wearied spirits.

Let us Englishwomen make a strong effort to rescue ourselves from this bondage, this constant drain on our resources; and, leaving to men the duty to the state, let us seek our work in what is our duty—the rule and guidance of the house, securing, as Ruskin says, "its order, comfort, and loveliness."

But especially must we insist upon its loveliness, which is the point most neglected in all that portion of our lives which does not lie immediately upon the surface.

THE REMEDY.

Bad habits to be reformed—Late hours—Value of the long winter evenings—Simplicity of manners—Over-carefulness—Instruction to be gained from foreign nations—Our manners should be natural—*Impedimenta* in our households—Comparison of former times with our own—Children trained to habits of consideration —Young men and boys over-indulged—Reduction of establishments—Lady helps—What is menial work?—Picturesque occupation—What is lady-like—Amateur millinery—Two subjects for an artist—Taste—Plan of the book—Eugénie de Guérin.

BEFORE speaking of work which has to be done in order to make our homes comfortable and beautiful, it is necessary to point out what ought not to be done.

We have fallen into one form of self-indulgence which goes far towards unfitting us for work, except under the stimulus of excitement. This is our national habit of keeping late hours.

This is an important matter, and one wherein

every member of every family may, if he pleases, aid reform. This, unless we are printers, bakers, or policemen, is entirely in our own hands.

Later hours are kept in England than in any other part of the world, and they grow later and later. We read in the life of the Prince Consort how painfully he felt this difference between England and Germany ; yet the latitude and climate of the two countries differ but little, and we are of the same race. It is merely a matter of custom.

Many persons pride themselves on breakfasting at ten o'clock, and nine is thought quite an early hour in comfortable houses. It is deemed aristocratic to breakfast late, as well as to dine late ; and as the day begun at ten o'clock would be too short for people to have a probable chance of sleep at ten at night, they are obliged to sit up till after midnight. Thus the best hours of the day are wasted, and the health of many injured by remaining an unnecessary length of time in a gas or paraffin laden atmosphere.

This shows an astonishing contrariety of disposition on the part of persons of refined sensations, so completely does it reverse the order of nature, which gives us the early sunshine for our enjoyment. Sunrise is the only beautiful natural spectacle that we modern English do not care about, except once or twice in our lives, when we get a shivering glimpse of it from an altitude of many thousand feet above the level of the sea.

From six to six is the natural day throughout by far the largest half of the globe, and the nearer we bring our practice to this measure the better; taking our day of sixteen hours (two-thirds of the twenty-four) from six o'clock in the morning instead of from nine. Old folks in the country ask their young people what is the good of sitting up burning out fire and candle. We never ask ourselves this question in London. Many persons take a nap after their heavy dinner, and only begin to feel lively as the clock strikes ten. To these the midnight oil is invigorating.

We have a valuable provision of nature in our long winter evenings, reckoning them at from five till ten. This gives us time for study, which we need more than do southern nations, to learn to contend against our climate. The northern peoples are famed for their mental culture : Scotland and Iceland bear witness to this. This is the season, too, for work in wool, to provide warm garments which are not required in the south. The wise woman does not fear the cold when her household is clothed in scarlet. This is the time when we may gather round the lamp or the fireside, and draw closer the family links under the influence of social warmth and progress.

Simplicity in our meals and dress is another point in which we may unite economy of money, time, and trouble, with comfort to ourselves and a regard for the beautiful. We need not drift into the carelessness of the picnic style of living, which is but the parody of simplicity. The real picnic is only suited to a few exceptional days in the year, and these our holidays. We may have simple meals indoors which should have all the freedom of picnic without its inconveniences.

Do we not all remember Swiss breakfasts with pleasure : the thyme-flavoured honey, and the Alpine strawberries ? Or, better still, those at

Athens, where the honey of Hymettus is nectar, and the freshly made butter ambrosia ; and our enjoyment of both was enhanced by the scent of the orange blossoms coming in at the open windows, and the sight of sunrise glowing on the purple hills? Or luncheons in Italy, under a pergola of vines, where a melon, macaroni, a basket of grapes, and a tricolour salad constituted the feast?*

These things dwell longer in our memories than does the aldermanic banquet.

Although every faculty need not be swamped in the gratification of the palate, our meals ought to give us pleasure. It is only when they are made of supreme importance that the satisfaction of a healthy appetite degenerates into mere greed, and what we call housekeeping means merely thinking of dinner.

Simplicity allows play (not work) to our higher faculties, which cannot be refreshed while we are overwhelmed with domestic cares.

* The tricolour salad imitates the Italian banner—red, white, and green. Green salad, beetroot, and cream, or white of egg whipped to snow.

" Martha was cumbered about," not with serving, but with too much serving. Doubtless, in the fulness of her hospitality, she tried to do too much, and so she showed irritability. Our Lord's teaching is always that there are good things prepared for us, which we cannot attain if we are overcareful and troubled about provision for the body.

There are roses in life for those who look for roses, if they will but give themselves time to gather them.

We may study with instruction and profit to ourselves the daily habits of foreign nations, and see where they fail, and also wherein they excel us.

M. Taine has put into words an observation which must have occurred to all of us who have travelled, how that " from England to France, and from France to Italy, wants and preparations go on diminishing. Life is more simple, and, if I may say so, more naked, more given up to chance, less encumbered with incommodious commodities."

From Italy we may go on to Arabia, and there see how little is used to keep the body in health. A woollen garment, warm enough to sleep in in the open air (we cannot say out of doors where there are no doors), and thick enough to keep off the scorching rays of the sun by day, and a thin shawl for. the head, is all their clothing; and the simplest meal once a day seems to be enough to keep them strong and active. Arabs have walked or run by my horse during whole days in the heat of the sun, and lived upon air until sundown, when they seemed to eat nothing but a little parched corn before stretching themselves down to sleep. It is not customary, even among the upper classes in Southern Europe and in the East, to eat more than two meals a day.

Liebig tells us of the nutrition of plants from the atmosphere : we may go further, and proclaim the nutrition of man from the atmosphere. On the moorland, on the mountain side, at sea, and in the desert, I have over and over again felt its feeding properties ; and we know that although we are, in such circumstances, hungry for our meals, we are not at all exhausted, nor do we want to feed frequently.

As the leaves of a plant absorb the carbon in

the air and give back the oxygen, so do we feed upon the oxygen and return the nitrogen. But we must have the oxygen. By our own present system of frequent heavy meals we throw all the hard work done by our bodies entirely upon the digestive organs, and when these are exhausted with their efforts, we feel faint, and mistakenly ply them with stimulants and concentrated nourishment, until at last they break down under their load.

But leaving the Arabs, who are types of a high race in a natural (uneducated) condition, may we not learn much from more civilized nations?

Besides taking example by the early hours of the Germans, we may imitate their industry, and, in our studies, their thoroughness and diligence of research.

From the bright, elastic French people we may (we women especially) copy their cheerfulness, frugality, and their keen, clear-headed habits of business. See how diligent they are at accounts, how quick at estimates, in ways and means; how they sharpen their wit, until it shines and makes their society sought as we in England seek a clever book. The Frenchwoman works the machinery of her own house, goes into the market and fixes the market-price of what she decides upon as suitable to her purposes (she always has a purpose, this Frenchwoman); she dresses herself and her children with taste, and she glitters in society.

From the Spaniards we may learn, by the warning of a proud race, what it is to sink into the scorn of other countries through smoking and debt.

From the Dutch we may learn cleanliness, from the Swiss simplicity, and from the Italians to foster our patriotism. Our American cousins are part of our own family; they only differ from us in having carried our virtues and some of our follies into the superlative.

We should endeavour to be natural in all our doings: to be ourselves, and not always acting a part, and that generally the part of a person of rank, or a millionaire. Let whatever we do be openly done, though not obtrusively nor boastfully; and this whether it is ornamental or only useful. To be truly ornamental it must combine utility. Is not the flower as useful as the leaf?

As an example of what I mean, I will give two

opposite instances. A young lady was making the bodice of a dress when a visitor called ; she quickly pushed the work under a sofa pillow, and caught up a gold-braided smoking-cap, half worked at the shop, which had lasted a long time as a piece of show-needlework.

The other case is that of a lady who set up for an example to her sex, and always displayed, as a manifestation of superiority, a basket full of gentle-men's stockings, which she seemed to be ever mending. Both of these ladies were acting a part.

Good taste has no false shame ; so we need not add the vexations of concealment to the accumula-tion of cares we have heaped upon our houses, till they are so encumbered with *impedimenta* of all kinds that our whole strength is taken to keep them in order, and the household machine has to move through such a mass of difficulties that it is like a loaded carriage lumbering through a Turkish road. Why should we add these things to life ?

We are daily bringing mechanism to greater perfection, and it is our own fault that we do not make it perform for our houses what Manchester has made it do for our looms, and render ourselves mistresses in reality, instead of merely in name, of our own households.

If we had to go back to the old flint-and-tinder-box days, when it was an hour's hard work in the dark to strike a light, when gas was unknown, when water was not laid on, when all bread must be made at home, all stockings knitted ; when there was no such thing as a ready made shirt, much less gowns and polonaises ; no perambulators, nor washing machines ;—we should not heap upon ourselves superfluous work in the thoughtless way we do at present, and then leave all to the attention of the most careless and irresponsible members of the community.

In a small family there is less work to be done ; in a large one there are more hands to do the work, and many hands make light labour.

We would have no mistress of a family a household drudge, while her daughters lounge over fancy-work or a novel ; but we would ease her hands, and uphold her in her true position of administratrix, mainspring, guiding star of the home.

Modern educational pressure causes too many of us to indulge our children, and release them from every personal duty. They must have time and quiet for their studies, and so they are allowed to become selfish, and to think that everything must give way to their mental improvement. Whereas we should train them to give as little trouble as possible ; and by good management, or by sacrifices, such as getting up earlier, to do at least the extra work appertaining to their individual enjoyment. Why should they, for instance, require hot water brought to their rooms several times a day ? Their grandparents used cold, and it was better for them. Why must girls have their hair brushed and braided for them ? Why must their lost gloves be found for them, and their wardrobes tidily arranged for them to throw into confusion in their hurry ?

Boys, especially, are so seldom trained to habits of consideration, that a young man in a house gives at least twice the trouble that his father does. Boys ring bells with intense heedlessness of its being some one's journey—oftener four journeys— to answer them. They make their boots unneces-

sarily dirty, and their other clothes also ; while the
extra baths on football days, and the cleansing of
the white garments, make many mothers wish the
noble game were not so popular ; and to sweep
up the dirt the boys bring into a house often
constitutes the chief work of a housemaid. We do
not expect boys to mend their clothes, but they
should be made to put them away, and to keep
their books, papers, and toys in their proper places,
and to take care of their own pets.

We excuse young men from doing these things,
instead of smoking or novel-reading through the
whole of their spare time, on the plea that they
work at money-making, forgetting that they do
so for themselves, and not, like their father, for
the family benefit. We might reform these things
materially, and remove much of the self-indulgence
which causes what has been truly called " the
shame of mixed luxury and misery over our
native land." If we all habitually gave less
trouble, we should require fewer servants to wait
upon us.

There is a scarcity of good working servants,

while the governess market is largely over-stocked. How many thousand of the poorest subjects of our Queen are now sinking, sick with hope deferred, into despondence, hating the present, dreading the future.

And yet on all hands we hear our lady friends say, "We must all wait upon ourselves now." The impossibility of finding the average of three servants for every house in London being now recognized. Why need there be three servants to every house, when servants are the greatest drain to the fortune of a family, worse even than the dress and society of its lady members, or than the tobacco of the men?

With study, and application of modern inventions, the three servants might be reduced to two; the two-servant-power establishments might dispense with one; and in many families where only one servant is kept, a lady-help would be found more useful, as well as more ornamental, than the " dolly-mop."

Trade is bad, and many young women, such as lace-makers, seek service. But being of the lower orders does not necessarily make them efficient servants, not more so than young ladies who have never learnt household work.

The existing puzzle is how to utilize the lady-help, for we must always bear in mind that she is a lady. She must not be merely ornamental, nor may we expect her to do anything menial. And here we must distinguish—this indeed is the great point for distinction—what is menial and what is not, and then see if we can reduce the number of works considered menial.

When we read of Marie Antoinette's delightful playing at work at the Trianon, and think of her in her bewitching costume, her work, the work she supposed herself to be doing, is placed in the region of picturesque poetry; as Tennyson's gardener's daughter, training her wreaths over the porch, is as poetical a personage as his pensive Adeline or stately Eleonöre.

We hear that the daughters of Queen Victoria take pride in, and give personal attention to, their dairies, and love to work among their gardens and model farms. And the Prince Consort

designed model cottages for the poor in which it
would be bliss to dwell, only it is impracticable to
make the poor endure novelties in domestic life.
Why, then, should we alone think it improper,
unlady-like, and what not, to study these everyday utilities, and plan improvements in sinks and
boilers?

But things are not so bad as they were thirty
and forty years ago, as regards what is lady-like
and what is not. We are emancipated from the
thraldom of its being considered genteel to be
idle, and interesting to be helpless, unable to dress
ourselves, or tie our own bonnet-strings without
the assistance of our maid. In my young days
we always had to wait for a maid to come and
hook our dresses; we should not endure this
now.

The favourite story of the Queen always putting
away her own bonnet, and folding up the strings (!)
helped much in sweeping away this fanciful
gentility. Since the introduction of the sewing-
machine, made as a piece of furniture fit for a
lady's sitting-room, ladies have been less ashamed

to be seen making their own dresses; and every girl now, of any pretension to taste, twists up her silk, tulle, and ribbons, mingling them in hats and bonnets with flowers or feathers, the most graceful objects in creation, until her skill produces a thing of beauty which is a joy throughout the summer.

What artist would desire a more charming subject for his picture than a pretty girl before her glass, trying in which position these delicate gauds best become the face they will adorn. It is holding nature up to the mirror. Yet some years ago girls were ashamed of a home-made bonnet, because their careful elders taught them it was more virtuous to make shirts than to cultivate their taste. The consequence was they were obliged to pay some guineas for a bonnet, as amateur millinery was a tissue of horrors.

The cooking-schools are helping us in another useful branch of housewifery. Here again woman's work is being raised out of the dulness of the "Berlin repository" into an atmosphere in which all the senses may revel. Smell and taste are here perfectly satisfied, and here we offer another picture for our imaginary artist—or perhaps the beholder may be a lover.

What more captivating sight than the girl of his heart deftly moving about among bright pots and kettles, and delicious bits of blue and other ware, gleaming among the copper stewpans?   Dutch tiles all round the stove, and everything as picturesque as in a Friesland kitchen (which we admire enough to go a long way to see), and the young housewife in a fresh and prettily worked dress of Holland or cambric, made short, showing her red morocco shoes, her sleeves short to the elbow, with a dainty bib and apron to keep her dress from soil : she rolling out pastry at a marble table, having by her side a graceful ewer of water, or fanciful milk-pot, and, in neat arrangement, quaint jars for jams, and pails and tubs of the carved wood which is so artistically made by the Norwegian peasants.   But I must fill up my outlines further on, as I enter into detail of each department of the house, and show how the first steps may be made easy in the direction of pleasant employment which shall be both useful and economical.

Do not look upon the taste and beauty of details as unimportant. They make up the harmony of our lives. Taste exercises a larger influence than we give it credit for. What makes Paris flourish? Why do we all enjoy it? Not for its Louvre galleries, nor for its intellectual life and culture most, but for its tasty shops!

We will speak of the house in the following order. First, the hall by which we enter it from the street; then we will bring our housewife into the kitchen, not necessarily, nor even advisably, downstairs, but near the entrance-door, so that the goods brought into the house need not have far to travel and be lifted (which would entail fatigue) before they reach the scene of their transmutation; the dining-room will come naturally next to the kitchen, as it should be nearest in a topographical sense.

Then we can adjourn to the withdrawing-room, and refresh ourselves with *jardinière* or conservatory before undertaking the arrangement of the bed-rooms and nurseries, where we pass so large a portion of our lives; and lastly, we will speak of the inhabitants, more particularly of the children. In considering the latter, we shall find the greatest benefit of anything I have recommended in this book, namely, that in place of the low-minded words and sentiments and vulgar habits of those who come nearest to ourselves in the society of our children, we may have a higher and purer association, so that the good of their future education will not have already been neutralized by corrupted early principles.

By interesting occupation our young ladies will have less time for sentimental troubles and fancied ill-health, which is nervousness. Eugénie de Guérin hit the mark when she wrote, "Yes; work, work! Keep busy the body, which does mischief to the soul! I have been so little occupied to-day, and that is bad for one, and it gives a certain *ennui* which I have in me time to ferment." On another occasion she speaks of having been writing and thinking, and then going back to her spinning-wheel or a book, or taking a saucepan, or playing with her dogs; and then she adds, "Such a life as this I call heaven upon earth."

THE ENTRANCE-HALL.

The evil of side doors—Difficulties with cooks—Who is to answer the door?—Four classes of applicants—Arrangements for trades-people—Visitors—Furniture of the hall—Warming the passages—Dirt and door-mats—The door-step— Charwomen.

MANY of the most respectable old houses in London and other large cities have only one street door and no area gate; and this is a great advantage, for of all inventions for the demoralization of households, the side or servant's door is the one which does its work· most surely. There is no oversight of it ; and neither master nor mistress can tell what is going on below-stairs, or at the back of the house, when the shutters are closed and the family are at dinner, or in the drawing-room in the evening.

The side door had its origin in a pride, or false shame, which could not bear to see a vestige of the working of the machinery of the house, and in that tendency to separate the ornamental from the necessary part of the household economy which has worked so disastrously for us all, making us, first, unwilling to take a practical share in the management of our houses, so widening the class division between mistress and servant; and secondly, has thrown us into such a state of dependence upon our subordinates that the boldest of us dare not venture into the kitchen except at stated hours ; and then, having received the programme of the proposed arrangements for the day from the cook, we are expected to go away and be no further hindrance to the eleven o'clock luncheon, which is one of the five solid meals daily required to sustain life in the hardships of service. Most ladies know what it is to wince under the sharp tongues of their cooks, who "don't like to have missuses come messing about in their kitchens," and their sarcasms upon " ladies who are not ladies," etc., etc., until many weak-minded victims retire before the enemy, and, giving up the vain pretence of ordering the dinner and examining the kitchen daily, send for the cook after breakfast, and get the interview over as soon as may be. It requires a very strong sense of duty to make one go where one is so palpably unwelcome, where one's most innocent looks are construed into a mean peeping and prying, and the least remonstrance is met by insolence.

I have, as a rule, been fortunate with my servants, and of late years I have successfully employed foreigners, who are generally more tractable than English servants.

I carried my point, when living in a villa near London, and locked the side door, retaining the key. I found great advantage in so doing on comparing notes with my neighbours, who told me their servants had threatened to leave directly there was a question of closing the side doors.

But this is only a recommendation where servants are kept. A responsible supervision of young servants is quite consistent with allowing them due liberty. This should always be granted them, as a dull imprisonment is misery to the young, and then they would not endeavour to take it in a clandestine manner, and surreptitious dealings with dishonest characters outside would be avoided.

To our present argument it matters little whether there be a side door or not, except that it affords greater facility to burglars ; so we will treat of the principal door as the only one, because this is most frequently the case in town-houses where there is no area gate, and the use of that does not enter into our plan of proceeding at all.

One of the first difficulties that presents itself to the lady wishing to maintain a small household staff is the opening of the front door. The question meets us on the threshold, who is to answer the door ? Who will be the slave of the ring ?

A lady-help does not like to undertake this office, and to the mistress it appears still more unsuitable. But let us analyze the subject.

There are four classes of people who knock at our door : the family, tradespeople, visitors, and casuals. The first division of the difficulty may be easily disposed of. The master and mistress, for these titles must be strictly maintained, have each a latch key ; the rest of the family may habitually use a particular knock agreed upon between them, and then the person who happens to be nearest to the door will open it.

Schoolboys and girls return at stated hours, and one is prepared for their appeal. For several years past my family has used four single knocks, which is a sign sufficiently unlike other knocks to be recognized immediately.

The postman's knock is well known, and in families where there is no great eagerness to get the letters, they fall naturally into the letter-box, which should be made deep, and the slit large enough to admit the *Times* newspaper easily.

In Italy it is usual to write the word *fuori* on a card, and stick it in the door when one is not at home ; and in this case visiting-cards would also be left in the letter-box. We might adopt this method, or even the Temple fashion of saying when we are likely to be home again.

The tradesmen are the most difficult to arrange for, and here invention must be called into play. Tradespeople first call for orders, and then with supplies.

Suppose we had our doors fitted with a kind of turnstile door, something like the birdcage gates which used to be at the Zoological Gardens, only with the outside made of wood, closely fitting, so as to admit no draught. This, by a push, would allow the goods to be deposited within the door, on the table upon which the cage turns round. The opening should be of a size to admit a leg of mutton easily. The goods, once deposited, could not be removed from the outside, as the door only works one way.

Through this opening the lady-housekeeper might give her own orders without their interpretation by an underling, and without being exposed to the public gaze, as she would be if the front door were fully opened, while the leg-of-mutton aperture would be sufficient for both parties to see to whom they were speaking. In the case of a single door, instead of the very general folding doors, it would be necessary to have the cage made to fold back, and the table to let down with hinges, to allow of the door being opened back against the wall; the table might be lowered after midday. This

arrangement would also dispose of most of the
casuals—the beggars, pedlars, and others who
haunt our door-steps—to the entire prevention of
hall robberies.

And now we come to the last and most considerable division of the subject—our visitors; comprising
relatives, friends, and strangers. If we lived in
Arcadia, or in the Colonies, we should most likely
be so glad to see our friends that we should joyfully
run to welcome them. Or if we were very great
people indeed, we should not mind doing as Queen
Victoria does, going to receive them at the moment
of their arrival. But as we are middling people,
and neither shepherdesses nor queens, we dread
being natural for fear of being thought poor.

For people are very much more afraid of being
thought poor than of being poor, seeing how often
they let themselves be dragged into poverty by
idleness and extravagance. The best remedy I
know for the fancied difficulty of opening our door
to our visitors, is to have no friends but those
whom we are glad to see, and to begin every new
acquaintance by putting it at once on a footing of

actual fact, letting people understand that we try to make the best of our means, and live within them. Then, if they will not take us upon our own terms, we need not regret that they do not wish for our friendship.

We shall find, in actual practice, that it makes very little difference to their opinion of us, if when we are at home we have the courage to tell them so ourselves; or if a dirty maid-servant, after an interval of waiting, receives their cards in the corner of her apron because her hands are black, and says she will go and see if "missis" is at home, or even if a neat parlour-maid fulfils the same office, and ushers visitors into a brown holland-encased room, leaving them to remark the time the lady of the house takes arranging her dress and her smiles previous to appearing.

In whatsoever way the ceremonial may be performed is of importance to none but ourselves. The visitor forgets it immediately, only retaining a general impression, cheery or dismal, as the case may seem; and if we are nice people and our visitors nice people, according to our respective ideas on that subject, we shall cultivate each other's acquaintance all the same.

It is immensely hard work to make five hundred a year look like a thousand. The effort to do so is seen through in an instant by a keen-sighted observer, and then it is ten chances to one if you get credit for what you really possess. It is never worth while to pinch and pare our everyday life for the sake of a few occasions of display.

Let us now go on to consider the best fittings and furniture for the entrance-hall.

Encaustic tiles make very good flooring for a hall, and are very easily cleansed with a mop or a damp cloth wrapped round a broom. A good thick door-mat is a great temptation to people to rub their boots well. This is really better than one of those delightful indoor scrapers all set round with brushes, which are seldom used after the first few weeks of their introduction. Mine is as good as new, and as highly polished, and I have had it for years. A couple of good door-mats are much more useful.

It is necessary to have a stand with a large drip-dish in a corner of the hall, to hang up cloaks and mackintoshes, and hat-pegs of course, but particularly a good-sized cupboard for boots, shoes, and goloshes, so that the family may change them in the hall on entrance. A carved *bahut*, or Italian linen coffer, is very useful in a hall for children to keep their school and garden hats and bonnets in, the lid serving for a bench ; but many halls, which are often merely narrow passages, would be inconveniently crowded by one of these rather ponderous pieces of furniture ; besides which, they are costly.

A deep bowl of Oriental china is as nice as anything for a card-dish, and the hall is a more appropriate place for it than the drawing-room.

Where it is thought necessary to warm the house, hot-water pipes laid from the kitchen are as cheap as anything. If the pipes are heated by a separate gas-stove in the hall, they will supply hot water to the bed-rooms also ; but it is not a healthy practice to heat the passages of a house : it causes the cold to be so much more felt on going out. Where the influence of the stove is felt in the bed-rooms it often prevents sleep.

E

In many houses which are kept too close and warm the families are subject to constant headache, and in others to a perpetual succession of colds ; according to their temperament requiring more oxygen, or their susceptibility to the sudden change from the heated to the outdoor air.

Unpolished oak is the most usual and the best material for hall furniture ; it is cleaned by rubbing with a little oil, which shows the grain and enriches its colour.

One rule which in practice saves more dirt in the house than any other, is that no member of the family be allowed to go upstairs in walking-boots. I have carried out this law for some years, after having long been troubled by my schoolboys rushing up and down stairs with their dirty boots on ; and the saving to my stair carpet is very considerable.   Boys and girls do not run up and down so often, if compelled to exercise a little attention beforehand.

But little boot blacking or brushing need be done in the house.   Gentlemen can easily have their boots cleaned out of doors, and ladies, by the use of goloshes, may reduce this work for themselves to a minimum, many kinds of boots being much better cleaned when sponged over lightly than when they are brushed or blacked. Every member of the family may not unreasonably be expected to take care of his or her own boots.

The door-step, or flight of steps, which is such an affliction to householders and such a joy to servants, may be kept sufficiently clean by being washed by the charwoman who comes one morning a week to do the scrubbing and scouring; which would be too menial—in other words, too public and too laborious—for any lady-help to endure.

Hearthstoning the step seems a very useless practice; the grey stone itself is a nicer colour, and only requires a mop or a broom to keep it free from dirt, according to the weather. Much white dust is brought into the house by the daily use of hearthstone, and precious time is wasted in the operation.

It may be well to understand, at the outset of our description of the work of a house, what parts of it cannot usefully or practicably be undertaken by

women who have been gently nurtured, before dis-
cussing the portions which their knowledge and
skill are best calculated to perform. For although
we may by forethought reduce within a small compass the toilsome part of the duties, there will
always remain some functions which it would use-
lessly tax a lady's valuable time and strength to
perform. For, after all, the office of the mistress is
to raise housekeeping to the level of the fine arts,
" where the head, the hand, and the heart work
together."

Incidental mention has already been made of the
charwoman ; she may be employed for the harder
work in the following manner :—

The charwoman should not have her meals in
the house, but she should be paid by the piece for
certain work done ; say, door-step, 1*d.* or 2*d.*, according to size and number of steps ; kitchen floor, 4*d.* ;
passages, according to size and requirements. Many
charwomen would gladly undertake work on this
plan, and many poor women or strong girls would
rejoice to do a morning's work and get home early
to their family with what would pay for their dinner

It is impossible to lay down fixed prices for piece-work, as this must necessarily vary with the size of houses and the habits of the owners.

The charwoman can shake the heavy door-mats, and sweep out the kitchen flue, if the species of stove used require sweeping—and most of them do. She may also break the large lumps of coal into knobs of the size necessary for the patent ranges needing fuel of a certain size, and she might place the week's supply of coal in the fuel-box.

It would be better in many cases to employ for this hard work a strong boy with a Saturday half-holiday. He could do it all quite as well as a woman, and much more easily ; but as we find we shall be taxed for a man-servant if we employ any arms but a woman's, we must make the best use we can of the worse means, consoling ourselves with the idea that the woman will use the money paid better than the boy might do.

BREAKFAST.

Lighting gas-fire—Difficulty of rousing servants—Family breakfast —Cooking omelet—Hours of work and enjoyment—Duties of mothers and householders—What is included in six hours' daily work—Clearing away the breakfast—Bowl for washing the *vaisselles*—Ornamented tea-cloths—Muslin cap worn while dusting—Use of feather-brush—Cleaning windows—Advantages of gas-fire.

THE gas-fire is the key-note of my system of domestic economy. The thing most impossible for a lady to contemplate doing, unless compelled thereto by duty, is to get up early, and before the shutters are open or the household stirring, to lay and light a fire, or light one already laid. The thought of going to a coal-cellar, shovel in hand, to bring in a scuttle of coals on a winter's morning is enough to make the bravest shudder. It is work only suited to those who have strength and hard nurture.

But can the most delicate woman think it a hardship to light the gas-stove, or tripod, in the dining-room, whereon stands an enamel-lined kettle ready filled overnight, or else a coffee-pot already full, and only waiting for the match to be struck to make it hot?

This is less trouble than to rouse one's self at seven o'clock to ring the bed-room bell, which often fails to summon a sleepy maid: and few English servants are early risers. Those who keep foreign servants have greatly the advantage in this respect.

Very many of us require our servants to rise and be downstairs before seven, as most gentlemen have to be in the city, or at their offices or chambers, by nine, and all schoolboys and girls at school. In the great majority of families breakfast must be ready punctually at eight.

While the family is assembling and prayers are being read, the kettle is boiling, and the tripod is soon ready for eggs to be boiled upon it, and bacon or kidneys fried.

My experience of another plan for a very comfortable every-day breakfast is, where a spirit lamp (methylated spirit, not petroleum) stands on the breakfast-table at the mistress's right hand, and from a plate containing eggs, butter, and some rashers of bacon, she cooks a savoury omelet, and fries the rashers in a small china fryingpan over the lamp, passing to each person the hot slices as they are done, and serving the omelet fizzling from the pan to all.

This process of cooking only takes five minutes, and the food is ready to be eaten as soon as the tea is made or the coffee poured out; and it is a pretty and cheerful occupation while letters are being read and talked of, or the *Saturday Review* cut.

A few savoury herbs, such as parsley or chives, are a great addition to the omelet; and it is easy to chop overnight the teaspoonful that is sufficient for the purpose, and put it on the plate with the other preparations. A few slices of cold potato are easily fried when the bacon is taken out of the pan; the bacon fat fries them deliciously. The china fryingpans may be bought at many shops, particularly at No. 9, Oxford Street, London.

Toast is not easily managed ; but with hot rolls from the baker's, marmalade, honey, and potted meat or ham, on the table, a very substantial breakfast may be had with little trouble, and no delay in its preparation.

We will suppose the gentlemen of the family have left the house for the business of the day, and the boys gone to school, and we will now, before continuing our description of the house and its furniture, give an outline sketch of the proceedings of the ladies during their absence.

For England expects every woman to do her duty, as well as every man, and to prove herself a help-meet for man before pretending to rivalry. The division of our time given in the old lines seems to be a very rational one—

> " Six hours to work,
> To soothing slumber seven,
> Ten to the world allot,
> And all to heaven."

This allows ample time for rest and enjoyment,

and sets apart an hour for daily service in the church for all who wish to attend it.

In Utopia, Sir Thomas More allots six hours a day for work to all men and women, and no longer ; as he holds it to be important that we should have more time available for enjoying the living we work for, than for working to sustain it.

We give ourselves so little enjoyment in our play, that a great man once said, " Life would be very tolerable if it were not for its pleasures." We have come to treat our play as if it were our work— and no wonder, since we have made it so very troublesome—and having thrown our appointed work upon the shoulders of other people, we now complain how badly they do it.

We mothers have a certain work given us to do, not by man, but by our Maker, whose servants we are. This is to take care of our children. Instead of doing this, we leave them almost entirely in the hands of strangers, and during great part of the day we know nothing of their doings, nor of what they are learning or thinking.

What should we say to a nurse or a governess

who neglected them as we do, and how shall we answer for our lack of care?

We householders have laid upon us the care of our houses. Yet it has come to be a recognized thing that we are to touch nothing in them with our own hands—at the utmost, we are to give our orders ; and the wealthy among us do not even do that, but are waited upon with every luxury, and then sent ready-dressed into society.

We are not our own, and we have little to do with the making of our position in life. We must accept the *status quo* and make the best of it ; so we may as well acquiesce cheerfully in our circumstances, doing as much as we can, and see if regular occupation will not make our hearts lighter, and help to bring back the days of Merry England again.

But we have no time for preaching now, and I would not willingly give a sermon in any case. I only threw out that suggestion of six hours' work for fear you might think I meant you to be busily employed all day, and then you would drop the book in disgust. But go on a little longer, and

you will find that I am less hard than the Ladies'
Art-Needlework Society, which insists upon eight
hours of close application, and far less hard than
the Cambridge Board of Examiners, which drives
you on night and day, leaving no time for household duties ; much less for dancing, or picking
flowers in country lanes.

No ; my six hours' work will include your music-
practising, and your attentive reading for purposes
of study. For unless yours be the only pair of
feminine hands in the family, you will not find
more than three hours occupied with household
work, and part of that time will comprise a daily
walk, a constitutional with an object, and the
remaining part will not be disagreeable ; at least,
I hope not, but it will be work and not play.

After this explanation let us return to our
subject. We will take it for granted that there are
at least two ladies at home. One, the lady-help or
eldest daughter, for example, will dust and set in
order the drawing-room, whilst the mistress of the
house proceeds to clear away the breakfast somewhat after the following manner.

When the coffee-pot was taken from the gas tripod to be placed on the breakfast-table, the kettle was refilled from a tap fixed on one side of the dining-room fire-place, and the water will be by this time hot enough to wash the cups and plates in.

Immediately under the tap stands a large bowl of Delft, or other ware sufficiently strong for daily use, and yet ornamental or picturesque enough to remain always in the dining-room. Terra-cotta is a good material for this purpose, as the colour is always decorative to a room. One might have a bowl of very elegant design made at the Watcombe terra-cotta works. Better still, in the case of its being required to be movable, would be a wooden bowl of the Norwegian carved work manufactured by peasant artists of Thelemarken, under the direction of M. de Coninck, of Christiania. Some one of Minton's vases or *jardinières* would answer the purpose very well ; but unless it had a plug and a pipe for letting off the water, like many washstands have, it would be heavy to lift with water in it. But a bowl with these fittings, placed on a fixed stand near the fire-place, would be well worth while taking some trouble to procure for the dining-room. It would be quite as ornamental, and no more expensive, than the china flower-pots on unsteady pedestals which are so universally popular ; indeed, it might balance one of these on the window-side of the fire-place, if it were thought proper. A piece of oilcloth might be spread under the pedestal, if it does not stand on the varnished floor.

From the sideboard-drawer will be taken a neatly folded tea-cloth, ornamented most probably with open work at each end, or adorned with colour in the style of the Russian household linen in the collection of the Duchess of Edinburgh, and the lady will proceed to rinse and wipe the breakfast cups and saucers, together with the teaspoons, milk-jug, and the cleaner plates, and will then lay the plates that have grease upon them to soak in the hot water, to which some additional hot water has been added.

Before taking out the plates, the china which has been used at breakfast should be neatly arranged on, or in, the sideboard. This saves the trouble of carrying about trays of crockery, and the consequent breakage. I will describe the china cabinet as I go more particularly into the details of the dining-room.

The remaining plates may now be wiped, and the *etceteras* replaced, the cloth brushed, neatly folded, and laid in a drawer with the table napkins, and the fryingpan cleansed by relighting the spirit-lamp for a minute while some hot water bubbles in it to clean it; the towel itself taken away to dry, and the tea-leaves, and a small basin of eggshells and scraps carried into the kitchen; the raw eggshells to be used to wash decanters and glass, and the tea-leaves reserved for dusting purposes.

The windows are opened and the gas fire turned out, and this important ceremonial of the day is at an end.

By this time the drawing-room will have been dusted by the second lady, the week's duster being kept in a convenient drawer. The feather-brush is wielded as a wand by the graceful mistress of the instrument, whom I should recommend to wear a muslin cap to keep the dust from falling on her hair.

These caps, when made of Swiss muslin and trimmed with a frill border edged with Valenciennes lace, are most becoming. They are best and prettiest when made in the shape of a large hair-net. A pretty bride used to come down to breakfast at Interlaken wearing this kind of cap, and other ladies at once adopted the style for wearing at their morning work or sketching. This was some years ago, but a good shape is always good.

To any one unused to the mysteries of dusting, it is surprising to find how easily the ornaments of a drawing-room may be kept in order, and how well the gilt frames of pictures preserved, by a light play of the feather-brush every morning. The French use the *plumeau* in nearly all cases where we rub with a hard duster, and with great advantage, especially in the case of gilding.

A man or woman hired once a month will keep the windows bright; they are all the brighter if

cleaned with newspaper dipped in cold water—
some mordant in the printer's ink has the property
of rendering them so—and they are the more easily
wiped, having less fluff about them than if cloths
are used.

A light rub with a leather makes bright stove
bars more brilliant, and in summer the fire-place
will give very little trouble ; though for ladies
managing their own work, andirons and a wood fire
will be found easier to keep in order, as well as
being more picturesque.

A gas fire, built with pumice and asbestos, lasts
without needing a touch for three years, and
though less delightful than wood or coal, is
infinitely cleaner, and gives no trouble at all. A
gas apparatus with four jets can be laid in any
ordinary fire-place, and fitted with pumice and
asbestos complete for seven and twenty shillings,
perhaps for less ; but that is what I have paid.
And when one considers the saving of labour in
carrying upstairs heavy scuttles of coal, besides
the original cost of the scuttles, with the ludicrous
inappropriateness of the ornamental varieties, the

F

total abolition of fire-irons, including that absurdity seen in many houses, the supplementary or deputy poker, besides requiring no chimneysweep in the drawing-room at all, it may be thought well worth while to have a gas fire laid at first. The superior cleanliness and security against smoke are great arguments for its general use, besides the ease with which it can be lighted, or turned out when not wanted for use. Being in the fire-place, the gas finds vent in the chimney, so there is no feeling of closeness in the room. The disadvantage of a gas fire, in some people's opinion, is that it may not be poked or touched ; but this is soon forgotten. Its appearance is like a clear fire of cinders, except when the sun is shining, and then it burns with a greenish tint not at all pretty.

Breakfast cleared away, and the drawing-room neatly arranged, the beds have next to be made. This is done with little exertion, as modern beds have spring mattresses, and French wool mattresses above these which require no shaking ; so that bed-making gives only a little exercise with a minimum of fatigue. Two people can make a bed with great ease, but as a rule I should advocate every person making his or her own bed.

I must not here go into the detail of setting the bed-rooms in order, as this will come more properly into the description of the upper part of the house. So I will only suggest that if one room be cleaned each day, and the staircase on one day, the house-work is not so heavy a task as it appears.

THE KITCHEN.

Parisian markets—No refuse food brought into a house—Catering
in London—Cooking-stoves—Pretty kitchen—Underground
kitchens objectionable—Kitchen level with the street door—
Larder and store-room—The dresser—Kitchen in the Swiss
style—Herbs in the window—Hygienic value of aromatic plants
—Polished sink—Earthenware scrap-dish—Nothing but ashes in
dust-bin—Soap-dish—Plate-rack—Kitchen cloths—Few cleaning
materials necessary—Hand work better than machine work—
Washing at home—Knife-cleaning—Fuel-box—No work in the
kitchen unfit for a lady to do.

TIME works many changes ; but will it ever bring
into our English markets the various and neatly
arranged vegetables, the bouquets of salad, pleasant
to the eye as to the taste, the neat little joints and
divisions of meat, the temptingly prepared poultry
and game, and the many kinds of appetizing
comestibles, which are to be found in the markets

of Paris? There a housekeeper may amuse herself
by varying her dinners for every day, having an
embarrassment of choice between countless delicacies. There the fillet of beef (the undercut of
the sirloin) is already larded for the roast; the
pigeons are boned and prepared for the *compôte*;
the veal is cut in shape and beaten for the cutlets;
the pigs'-feet are boned, stuffed, and truffled; slices
of galantine are ready to be laid on a dish for
luncheon; crayfish woo the *mayonnaise;* parsley
and butter are waiting to be poured over potatoes
à la maître-d'hôtel. There the spinach may be
bought ready boiled and finely chopped, only
needing to be warmed with its poached eggs; the
sorrel is already picked over and cooked; the
carrots are cleanly grown, and evenly selected, and
sold with just the quantity of feathered green tops
useful for a garnish. In fact, all is so contrived
that the least possible refuse matter shall be
brought into any house, so saving the labour that
this entails.

Nor does this trimming and spoke-shaving add
to the price of the articles, as the surplus vegetable

remains go into the ground at once, but little of what is uneatable being taken to the market at all ; thus saving the cost of carriage, and paying for the little time expended in its removal ; while in the case of meat, the purchaser finds it more profitable to cook only such parts as are entirely eatable, without letting time and fire be consumed in preparing what is always wasted.

This is not a cookery-book, though when I think of how much we have to learn before we can make good use of our fine provisions, I feel tempted to branch off on this line ; but the lady amateur will learn more by giving careful attention at the cooking-school than by reading many books.

In London we can buy peas ready shelled, fowls ready trussed, fish prepared for the pot or pan, and sometimes our beans ready slit ; but carrots must be scraped, greens washed, and turnips peeled, and apples also, though potatoes need not; tongues and hams may be bought boiled, and cakes ready baked. Still, with us much more food has to be prepared at home than in France, though we have this convenience—that the provisions are brought by the tradesmen to our doors, which is seldom the practice there.

For general cooking, the gas tripod like that used at breakfast will not serve our turn, except on cold-collation days in the heat of summer, when cold lamb or salmon, salads and fruit, are more grateful than anything else.

Many people dislike to have their cooking done by gas, and it is objectionable for roasting or broiling; still, there are such numerous inventions in cooking-stoves, each simpler, cleaner, and more perfect than the rest, that only the embarrassment of selection can cause hesitation in making a choice.

Near a nice bright stove, placed in a recess glittering with Dutch tiles or Minton's artistic *plaques*, surrounded by burnished pans and pots of well-lined copper or brass and neat enamelled saucepans, the genius of the hearth presides over the mysteries of Hestia.

The window, made with diamond panes mingled with a few lozenges of bright colour, is mostly open in summer, and wreathed with climbing plants—as

vines, and ornamental gourds, with their curious
black or scarlet fruit, the rich foliage intercepting
the sunshine—or closed if it be winter, and draped
in pleasant muslin. I would take great pains to
make my kitchen the most picturesque and cheerful room in the house, as it is one of the most
important.

On no account would I use the great black
beetle-trap cellar downstairs and underground,
which strikes with dismay the greater number
of young girls who have rushed from school into
marriage, and who instantly become the prey
of the tyrant imprisoned in that dungeon, which
is too often also a den of iniquity.

No ; if obliged to have a house with one of these
dismal caverns, I would invent some useful purpose for it ; but I would not willingly select such
a dwelling. These underground kitchens must
eventually die out, and our children will wonder
why we used such airless, lightless places.

In a house arranged on my plan we aim up-
wards, not downwards. We might, perhaps, on
wet days, let the children go to these basement

rooms to skip or romp, as there they could not shake down the ceiling beneath them, as sometimes happens in upstairs play-rooms; only the rooms must be kept carefully whitewashed, and, as far as possible, well aired.

Or the old kitchen might be fitted up with racks for guns and fishing-rods, and used as a smoking-room, when cosily papered, and carpeted with matting; and the back kitchen converted into a carpenter's shop with lathe and tool-chest.

But our kitchen, the pride of our house, will be level with the dining-room and front door. It is a foolish practice to have all vegetables, meat, coal, etc., taken downstairs for the purpose of bringing then all up again.

When it is impossible to spare two rooms on the ground floor for household use, let both kitchen and dining-room be upstairs, while the drawing-room might be on the ground floor. This would give no more work than does our present custom. But where it is possible, it is better, for obvious reasons, that the kitchen should be on a level with the street door.

When the room used as kitchen is large and has two windows, one side of it may be partitioned off for a larder, or store closet; or if there is a small third room near, it may be used for these purposes. But much depends upon the aspect of the room and its means of ventilation. A town larder need not be large, as the butcher, fishmonger, etc., can keep the provisions far better than we can do in the best of larders. A pantry and scullery will be quite unnecessary in a house arranged in this way. Wine will be kept in the usual wine-cellar, but beer, in bottles or in a small cask, may be kept in the cupboard under the stairs which is so universal in town houses.

The kitchen floor should not be carpeted; but one or two undyed sheepskins make comfortable mats, and are easily cleaned.

The kitchen dresser may be made of the usual shape, though the cornice seems superfluous, as it is too high for anything but dust to rest upon it.

Where it is thought better to do so, the old kitchen dresser may be brought bodily upstairs. If it is varnished and its back painted red, and the edges of its shelves very dark brown, with bright brass hooks in them, it may have bright brass handles put on its drawers, and it will do very well ; and white or blue-and-white ware will look extremely well upon it.

A kitchen may be very prettily fitted up in the Swiss style, with unpainted deal employed decoratively whenever there is a fit occasion for it. The back of the dresser may be made of narrow boards, each lath cut out uniformly in a pattern at the top, forming a band of ornament. The shelves will look very nice with a border of fret-work, in sycamore, placed either above or below their edges. They are more easily cleaned if the ornamental border is fastened on like barge-boarding, but this plan is not so well adapted for hooks.

Mottoes in old English character, which is similar to the German Gothic type used in Switzerland, form an appropriate decoration to the cornice of the room.

The tables and chairs must be of unpainted wood, plain, but of good form. All hooks and bars, or whatever cannot conveniently be made of wood,

should be of wrought iron.   This gives a good
opportunity for having window-bars and fastenings,
or even a balcony, made in ornamental iron work.
The window-curtains will be of Swiss muslin.

Oval wooden pails, with a board on one side left
tall and cut out for a handle, made in various sizes
for water, milk, etc., are as useful as they are suitable to the style adopted ; and baskets may be
made like those carried by the Swiss mountaineers
at their backs.   A cuckoo clock and a few hooks
of chamois horn carry out the effect. Characteristic
ornaments, such as paintings of Swiss scenery,
and flowers in wooden frames, wood carvings on
brackets, wooden bears as matchboxes, wooden
screw nutcrackers, should be collected during visits
to Switzerland ; and a Swiss costume will be found
as practically useful as any dress the young cook
can wear, and will add a great charm and liveliness
to the scene.

But be the style adopted what it may, and it
is well to exercise individual tastes, it need not be
made expensive, or not more so than an ugly
kitchen.   Thought and care should combine to

make it cheerful and attractive, in order that the
real work to be done in it may not have a depressing influence : that the lady, or her assistant,
may not pine for the greater excitement of the
Row or the rink. The kitchen window should be
well furnished with scented plants; and in case
of having no garden, pots of parsley, mint, and
thyme may be grown successfully on a balcony.
Every house might possess its sweet basil plant,
and every Isabella might rear it in as elegant
a pot as that in Holman Hunt's picture. Plentiful
use should be made of it in cookery; it is one of
the best of herbs. Indeed, we too much neglect
all these aromatic plants, the hygienic value of
their fragrance alone being very great. Some girls
might save the small fortune they now spend in
opopanax and patchouly, by cultivating lavender
and thyme for their wardrobes; while balm and
bergamot are sweet enough to make the kitchen
smell like Araby the Blest.

China ginger-jars will be found good for preserving dried herbs for winter use.

The sink is a very important part of the kitchen

furniture. This, in our model kitchen, should be a shallow bath of Marezzo marble, which is a strong, durable composition, finely coloured. We should select it of a colour harmonizing with the general style of the kitchen. The sink must rest upon two columns, or short shafts, of the Marezzo marble, hollowed down the centre, to allow of the water running freely away at both ends of the sink, each tube being stopped by a bell-trap. It must stand on one side of the kitchen fire-place, so that a pipe and tap may readily communicate with the self-supplying boiler. There must also be the usual pipe to conduct cold water from the cistern.

The best possible sink would be of real marble, highly polished ; but the cost of this would preclude its use in our economical household. Enamelled slate would be cheaper and very good, and it would retain its polish better than the Marezzo marble, or japanned metal might answer the purpose pretty well. But doubtless a demand for such articles would cause Messrs. Minton's factory to produce a sink in strong glazed earthenware which should be finely coloured as well

as elegant in form, making, indeed, an object as
beautiful as a Roman porphyry bath. Many of
the public washing fountains in Italy, or the south
of France, would serve as models for this purpose.
One of the most important points to be attended
to is that it should be highly polished, as grease
would be more easily removed from it, and it
would be cleaner.

Beneath the sink is the pot for scraps and refuse,
of which a small quantity is inevitable, unless there
is a garden, or poultry are kept; in which cases
all rubbish may be turned to account, the only
exception being fish-bones and scraps, which, under
all circumstances, must be burned.

The refuse dish should be of earthenware to
match the sink, or of terra-cotta, glazed inside.
It must be made in two compartments, one for
usable scraps and one for waste. Each division
should have a cover with a small air-hole in it,
both covers made sufficiently heavy not to be
upset or opened by the cat ; and there must
be a handle to lift it out once a week, or oftener,
when its contents are disposed of, either as gift,

or to some person calling for it regularly. In all economical families the dripping is consumed either for frying, or else clarified for cakes, etc. Cinders, of course, are to be sifted in the covered cinder-sieve, and the ashes only allowed in the dust-bin. By care on this point, seven-tenths of all fevers might be prevented.

By the side of the sink should stand a neat towel-horse for drying the damp cloths; and a pretty dish made in two divisions, with a strainer for soap and soda, should be hung in a convenient place. This dish would be best made in earthenware, but it might be of carved wood in a kitchen fitted up in the Swiss style.

A plate-rack must be above the sink, and here is great scope for tasteful decoration without interfering with its lightness or strength. A rack like those in general use would, however, be perfectly inoffensive, and so would our ordinary buckets and dish-tubs; but souvenirs of travel, such as the quaint wooden pails seen at Antwerp, or the brass fryingpan-shaped candlesticks at Ghent, should be eagerly sought, as they add much to the picturesqueness and piquant liveliness which are so desirable.

A round towel, on a roller with nicely carved brackets, is indispensable. This should be of finer holland than it is generally made of, being for ladies' use; or it might preferably be of soft Turkish towelling, with coloured stripes and a fringed end, and so be pleasanter to the eye and touch than the ordinary jack-towel.

The dresser-drawers must have their piles of kitchen cloths neatly folded, and separated for their different services. These should be the pride of the young housewife's heart, all of them having their ends tastefully ornamented, either ravelled out or knotted into fringe for the commonest, or open worked, or edged with Greek lace and *guipure-d'art*, according to their quality; the dusters only being plain, and these of two sorts, one stout for furniture, and the other kind of soft muslin for ornaments. Housemaid's gloves, wash-leather, and any favourite cleaning materials, should be kept in a drawer by themselves; but in my experience I have found very few of these

G

things necessary. As is the case with all the arts, the more complete the paraphernalia, the less is the work done. It takes so long to set in order one's apparatus, and to play with it a little, that as soon as something is begun to be done, it is time to put all away again. How often we see this with amateur painters; they set out too heavily equipped.

The black-lead and brush, and broken saucer full of something pulpy, the powder that is always falling out of its packet or bit of newspaper, and the other odds and ends which crowd our house-maids' dirty buckets, and the scrubbing brushes and hearthstone which encumber our sinks, are only barbarisms trying to conceal the slovenliness they pretend to correct. A house regularly and neatly attended to needs few or none of these things, while sandpaper, rotten-stone, and whiting may be almost entirely dispensed with. The homely old proverb should be remembered, when tempted by advertisements of these things, " Elbow-grease is the best furniture polish."

Mincing-machines, apple-paring-machines, and

toys of this kind, are all very well when ladies use them themselves; but they represent so much idleness, waste, and destruction in the hands of careless cooks, who like to sit over their letter writing, or their weekly paper, while the kitchen-maid does the work. And when a fragile machine breaks or gets out of order under her heavy hand, she only "drats the nasty thing" and throws away the broken part, pushing the rest aside to become a portion of the dreadful accumulation of lumber to be seen in every house.

My own practice as a wood-carver teaches me to prefer using that perfect tool, the hand, in its ever adaptable way, to using it servilely to grind out sausages. By the time one has prepared the meat to feed the machine, set it in working order, and taken it to pieces again to clean it, one might as soon have used a sharp knife, and the meat would have tasted better than it does when its juice is squeezed out and its fibre torn to rags, so that the insipid *rissoles* made from it need half a bottle of Harvey's sauce to make them eatable. It may be a matter of taste, but the difference seems to me as great as between music played on a piano and noise ground out of a barrel-organ.

Washing-machines, I have found to my cost, are a failure also, at least in hired hands. I bought one of the best, but as I had also a washing-tray, the machine, warranted to do everything, was neglected, and its lid employed as a table ; as we too often see with our pianos, telling thereby a tale of forgetfulness. The mangling part of the machine, which was sometimes used by semi-compulsion, always had its screw left turned on at full pressure, so that the spring would have been powerless in a week, had I not loosened it myself. Washing at home had better not be attempted in the case of ladies doing their own work. We want to lighten the labour of the house ; since, if we endeavour to do too much, we shall either become household drudges, or else decline the work altogether.

But supposing a family has time and opportunity to do the laundry work at home, a tablespoonful of liquid ammonia and a dessertspoonful of turpentine used in the washing water, where a quarter of a pound of soap has been finely sliced, will be found to remove dirt from the clothes without rubbing, saving labour, much soap, and the wear and tear of the things.

In the case of large families, besides the greater economy of washing at home, which is, however, doubtful when extra labour is hired, the immunity from infectious diseases being brought home in the linen is a powerful motive for undertaking the work, and doubly so where there is a garden, as it is so much better for our health to wear linen dried in the fresh air, rather than in the small courts of the neighbourhood where our laundresses usually dwell, or in the close passages of their houses.

Kent's patent knife-cleaner is as much used, and as useful, as any of these domestic machines, though I prefer the leather-covered board. Pyro-silver knives seem to save labour, as they are cleaned like any spoon; wiped first, as all greasy knives should be, with paper, then washed in warm water and wiped with a cloth. My own pyro-silver knives keep very well and remain bright, but as they have valuable handles of elaborate Burmese ivory-carving they are carefully used. I have heard people say that the pyro-silver does not wear well, being easily scratched and otherwise injured.

Balancing the sink on one side of the stove is the fuel-box, containing a quarter of ton of coal. This, in most of the new stoves, will last several weeks, and it may be bought in this small quantity at a time, or replenished from the usual coal-cellar. This consideration would be determined by the season, by whether the other stoves in the house burn gas or coal, and by the number of rooms requiring daily fires.

The fuel-box should have a lid, forming a table for any temporary uses, or any of the less cleanly sorts of work—I will not say dirtier work, because in this system there should be no dirty work, nothing but what a lady may do without loss of dignity, and without injury to hands which in the afternoon will handle delicate needlework, and in the evening recreate themselves over the piano.

And this leads us to speak of the systematic employment of lady-helps, in such cases as they may be a real comfort and assistance in a family, and not where they are expected to be perfect servants, who for small wages will relieve idle ladies from the difficulty of first obtaining and then enduring a few ignorant domestics.

THE LADY-HELP.

True position of a lady-help—Division of work in a family—The
mother the best teacher — Marketing — Young lady-helps—
Luncheon—Early dinners for children—Recreation—Preparing
the late dinner—Evening tea—The lady-help a gentlewoman—
Her assistance at breakfast—Her spare time—Tact.

I USE this title, not because I think it is the best,
but because it is already in general use; though,
as yet, very few people have any clear idea of
what the true position of a lady-help should be.
Some persons suppose they must treat her as a
visitor, in which case she would be worse than
useless, and such a situation could not possibly
be permanent. Others think she must be employed precisely like an upper servant, and only
look upon her as a means of escape from the
penalties of their own position.

In houses where there are grown-up daughters

it is not necessary, nor even advisable, to employ any labour outside of the family beyond that of the charwoman, as previously described.

The work may be so divided as to press too heavily on none, always bearing in mind, however, that, as "Life is real, life is earnest," there is real work to be done in every household, the aim being to lighten it by contrivance, and by utilizing modern inventions; in fact, making of science and social economy two valuable servants, instead of exalting them to be our masters, as we have all been doing lately. For, notwithstanding all our brilliant inventions, we have so multiplied our wants that life is neither easier nor cheaper than it was in the days when we knitted our own stockings, spun our own flax, and used strong handloom sheetings, and woollen cloths which were not made of shoddy.

Let us take as a typical family a mother and three daughters, two of them grown up and one still a child—a by no means uncommon instance. The men and boys may be many or few, it makes little difference to our example.

Probably the mother is not so strong as the grown-up daughters. She might make choice of the needlework department, or the teaching, supposing her own education to have been good ; in which case she would add the benefit of her experience to every lesson given, rendering it far more valuable than instruction from a young teacher ; as in all branches of study she would distinguish what is good and lasting from what is merely ephemeral, and we should have fewer flimsy pieces of music learnt to the exclusion of great masters, and fewer meretricious drawings on tinted paper, as we grow out of our admiration for these things at an early period, and home education would have a more solid groundwork. Young teachers are too apt to think they know everything, and only aim at their own standard of education, finished as they believe it to be.

Perhaps the mother might prefer to reserve a general oversight, with only such lighter work as the breakfast-table as already described. The daughters could share the remaining work in the following manner.

While the breakfast is being cleared away, one daughter, accompanied by her youngest sister, will arrange the bed-rooms, and dust the drawing-room and such parts of the dining-room as have not been included in the work of setting in order after breakfast. The little girl would rejoice in helping in this way—all children do ; and when they have no real work of this kind, they imitate it with dolls' houses. Housekeeping is one of a girl's natural instincts ; it is only quenched by accomplishments being put in its stead.

While the manager of the needlework sees what requires her attention in that department, and plans it for unoccupied hours—keeping, perhaps, some fancy portion of it for pleasant work in the evening, while music or reading is going on—the daughter who is housekeeper for the week attends to the culinary arrangements, and considers what marketing will be required. She will, either alone or accompanied by one of her sisters, proceed to give her orders at the various shops, or go to the market and make her own selection. She will bring home some of the purchases herself

—any parcel, for instance, that is no heavier than a little dog—but mostly the things will be sent to the house.

Co-operative stores may or may not be an advantage to their customers—it is a disputed point; but two good things they have done for us: first, making us pay ready money for what we buy; secondly, doing away with the ridiculous fear we formerly had of being seen carrying a parcel.

This expedition will have given our young heroine the necessary morning air and exercise, and it need not be so long as to prevent her enjoyment of a more ornamental walk in the afternoon—visits, or a cruise in the rink.

In the case of there being only one grown-up daughter, a young lady-help may be thought an agreeable addition to the family. She would be a pleasant companion to the daughter, and they might share the work in the same manner as two sisters would do. If she were more accomplished, or better read, than the daughter of the house, this would be a source of improvement to the latter ; or if the superiority were on the other side, the benefit resulting to the companion would be such as to make her endeavour, by increased usefulness, to show her sense of the advantages whereby she would be enabled to add to her acquirements.

Much ease in daily life is obtained by dining early ; but as this is seldom possible where fathers and husbands are out all day at their employments, the necessarily late dinner involves a sacrifice of our time and pleasure, which we must try to render as small a hardship as may be, and take as a duty what is such in reality.

Luncheon for ladies is easily provided where there are no ravenous schoolboys and girls to cater for, because, as they will dine late, the luncheon need not be a hot spread meal. A tray with slices of cold meat, bread, butter, cheese, or perhaps some cold potatoes fried, or any easily warmed little dish remaining from yesterday's dinner, will make an ample luncheon, with a glass of beer or some claret. But if there are schoolboys and girls who come home to an early dinner, it is indispensable that it should be a real dinner, and no make-believe. The experience of schools and large families shows us that the cheapest and most wholesome fare for children is a joint of meat, with potatoes and another vegetable, a daily pudding, varied according to circumstances, bread, and beer. No adjuncts; neither pickles nor condiments, cheese nor dessert. All these *etcetceras* are superfluous and unwholesome, and entail extra plates and additional trouble to everybody.

The joints of meat, with potatoes and Yorkshire pudding, are as well cooked at the baker's as at home, and with much saving of heavy work.

The following is a good working-plan for a large family : a joint of meat roasted the first day, the next day cold, which is better for the children than having the joint cut in two and both parts eaten hot—cold meat is very good for them. The remainder may be stewed, or otherwise warmed up on the third day; and so forth, varied with boiled meat occasionally and fish once a week—on Friday in preference, as there is a better choice of it on that day, it being purveyed for the Roman

Catholics and others who eat it on principle. Monday is the worst day for fish.

The daily pudding should be simple, without sauce, and with very little spice. Spices become valuable medicines when not habitually taken with the food.

It is a mistake to feed children entirely on meat and potatoes ; this diet does not afford sufficient variety. Fruit and milk puddings are very wholesome and nourishing for children, and so is simple pastry, when made without baking powder, the frequent use of which is very lowering, as is the case with all alkalies.

Luncheon over, the hours from two till half-past four are free for everybody. Now is the time for music-practice, walks, visits, and general recreation.

Visitors drop in about this time, and may be encouraged to stay by the sight of the afternoon tea-table standing ready arranged in a corner of the drawing-room. The descent for five minutes of one of the ladies will be sufficient time to make the tea and produce a plate of biscuits, or the cake-basket. The gas may be lighted under the kettle at the time the door is opened to visitors.

At half-past four the fire must be made up in the kitchen, and all things put in readiness to prepare the late dinner. This, in the interest of the health of all, and especially of those who return home tired and hungry, should not be later than six o'clock, where it is possible.

The dinner and dessert occupy little more than an hour, and half an hour is sufficient to clear all away, and set the things ready for the next morning's breakfast. The cloth may be left spread on the table, only brushed and neatly laid.

We have then a pleasant social evening left us ; two hours and a half before ten o'clock, which may or may not be broken by an evening cup of tea, according to taste.

Luxurious people, whose days hang heavily on their hands, are the fortune of the doctors. Among them we may include servants in large houses, who are, perhaps, more self-indulgent than any. And it is the habitual five meals a day

required to fill up time in an opulent house, that
contribute most to fill the pockets of the physician.

It is pleasant, certainly, for an occasional change,
to stay in a house where at nine o'clock the butler
and two footmen stalk in with the tea-tray and its
appurtenances ; but the main, though unacknow-
ledged, cause of the ceremonial is, that it may be
seen that the men-servants are at home in the
evening, and not at the public-house.

As a daily habit, however, the continual breaking up of time caused by the ever-recurring meals
is very tiresome to those whose occupations are so
unnecessarily hindered.

It has been shown that the daily housework for
a small family is not too arduous to be undertaken by the members of that family, in any case
where the grown-up ladies in the house are two or
more. But in the circumstance of a young wife
and mother, it were better that she should not
attempt to cope with the greater part of the household work, especially if she be alone in the house
all day, or with young children only. The sense

H

of solitude is too depressing, and all unshared labour is much heavier.

In case of her having no sister, or female friend or relation, to whom she might be glad to offer a home, she should seek a cheerful lady-help, who would be pleased to feel she is putting her time to profit. And if strong, healthy, and a skilful manager, the lady-help will find how far more interesting this varied work may be made, than the drudgery of sitting in a dreary school-room as governess to a tribe of tiresome children, where her only recreation is the monotonous daily walk ; or the more independent, but far more laborious, occupation of a fine-art needleworker, to whom eight hours' continuous daily toil are obligatory.

As far as I can see and judge by letters written to the *Queen* and other papers, and the jokes in *Punch*, the difficulty, almost impossibility, of getting gentlewomen as helps is the drawback to their being put forward as a solution of the domestic difficulty. The engagement of half-educated or pretentious daughters of small tradespeople is by no means desirable, either for themselves or for us.

We do not wish them to be our companions, yet they must be treated with a greater degree of familiarity than ordinary servants ; and if they are allowed to be on a nominal footing of equality, it can only tend to lower the tone of the whole household. But the lady-help, in an establishment suited to the feelings of such an one, may easily be a gentlewoman by birth and education, and not a lady in name merely.

As regards the invasion of domestic privacy, which has ever been found such a disadvantage where a companion, or a governess, is always the sharer of our meals and conversation, it is by no means necessary, hardly even possible, that this should be the case with a lady-help ; except at breakfast, when it is surely no hardship, but the contrary—indeed, it must be a pleasure—to have at our children's most important meal the assistance of a lady whose care of their wants prevents our own breakfast being uncomfortably hurried.

For breakfast is unlike dinner-time in this, that as husband and wives have already had plenty of time for all they wish to say to each other, the presence of a third person is not inconvenient, while at their reunion about dinner-time, when each has the day's adventures to relate and comment upon, a stranger is sometimes in the way.

Indeed, it is one of the greatest difficulties in the lady-help system, that of necessity she cannot sit at table while serving the dinner.

The greater number of ladies will be as well pleased to have their spare time for their own pursuits, as to be obliged to sit in the drawing-room all the evening, trying to seem amused with doing nothing. A lady offering herself for work of this kind will generally be of an energetic temperament, and able to employ her leisure profitably in reading, drawing, or needlework, or perhaps she may have her own piano in her room.

It would frequently conduce to the comfort of all parties if she had an invitation, which she might accept or refuse, to join the drawing-room circle; and this should be given on occasions when it is likely to be agreeable to her, at such times as her necessary duties will cause no awkwardness to herself, the mistress, or the guests.

Exercise of tact will be frequently called for, no doubt, in this avowedly the weak part of the scheme ; but with wit, invention, and a hearty endeavour to make a subordinate position as little painful as possible, many difficulties will be tided over, and when once the novelty of the method is worn off, many little complications, by being less thought of, will be less felt.

Where a governess is kept as well as a lady-help, the two ladies could enjoy life together quite independently of the general company ; and it might be found perfectly compatible with their avocations to give them permission to invite their personal friends to spend their evenings occasionally with them.

In the case of the daughters of the house taking its duties upon themselves (and no one can consider it an ungraceful service to wait upon a father), the way would be smoothed by common endeavour of all the members of the family, and much kindly courtesy would be aroused, and earnest effort to give the least possible trouble ; all of which should be done in the case of the lady-help.

When we go more deeply into the detail of the dinner, which is the *pièce de résistance* of the day's programme, we will endeavour to show how, by careful fitting and steady guidance, the wheels of the domestic machine may run smoothly and noise- lessly in their grooves, especially if the oil of good humour be plentifully supplied.   And several sug- gestions will be offered, which, however, must be looked on merely as suggestions, and not as essen- tial parts of the system ; for in every household there will be modifications, according to the in- finite variety of tempers, tastes, and habits of the family.

THE DINING-ROOM.

HAVING given a sketch of the kitchen, I must now
fill up that of the dining-room, which we left after
the breakfast was cleared away.

As the gas-tripod, the spirit-lamp, and the large
bowl for washing the china and other crockery
have been already described, we may proceed to
consider what more immediately relates to the
dinner-table ; since the rest of the furniture need
not materially differ from what is at present in use.

In selecting a carpet for the dining-room, let us

remember that a Brussels carpet is more easily brushed and kept clean, than are Turkey or Indian carpets.

If it be made with a border, and the floor stained and varnished all round at a width of from one to two feet from the wainscot, beside being cheaper to begin with than a fitted carpet, it is more artistic in appearance, and more readily taken up periodically to be beaten; while a long brush easily dusts the varnished margin, and a damp cloth tied over a harder broom will wash it in case of necessity. Bordered square carpets are the more durable, as they are able to be turned round as one part becomes unduly worn.

The best kind of curtains for a dining-room are of some rich-looking woollen stuff, thick enough not to require lining. Rep is very serviceable, but there are many more curious foreign fabrics which may sometimes be met with at no very great cost.

Curtains ought to run easily on a pole, either of wood or metal. If of metal, it should not be very large, as the size of a hollow rod does not add to its strength. Curtain rings can be sewn on at home, and so can any cord that may be thought desirable at the edge, though this does not often improve curtains from an artistic point of view. There is no need of the upholsterer's intervention, which mostly doubles the price of the curtains.

The height from the floor to the top of the window should be measured, and the requisite number of yards of material bought, allowing a margin for curves in the folds of the drapery. The rods should be sufficiently long to allow the curtains to hang entirely upon the wall, not over-hanging the window in the least. This preserves the drapery, and keeps it from fading, while it does not exclude the light.

The curtains should be ample enough to cover the window completely when the shutters are shut, without leaving a streak of opening. They should likewise extend to the ends of the pole, so as comfortably to keep out the draught.

If muslin curtains are used, they may conveniently be tacked inside the woollen ones about half-way ; this will keep the latter from some dust. A few additional rings can be slipped on the pole, to which the remaining central parts of the muslin will be gathered.

Curtains should touch the floor, or nearly so, but they need never be allowed to lie in heaps on the ground, as was formerly the fashion ; and the voluminous folds sustained by brackets have been advantageously exchanged for a simple band to hold back the curtain.

Our mothers and grandmothers were certainly victims to their upholstery ; we have improved in this respect. It does not take many minutes to unhook our curtains, shake them free from dust, and hang them up again; we have no com-plicated pulleys to get out of order perpetually, nor ponderous cornices with heavy valances, and wonderful gimp and fringe. Those were fine times for the upholsterers !

Do not hang your dining-room pictures very high ; few of us tower above six feet, and it is easier for those who do so to stoop, than for the rest of us to stand on tip-toe ; we must consider the convenience of the majority.

Money is well expended on picture-frames, as

when they are handsome and chosen with taste, they enhance our enjoyment of the pictures. But a costly frame is not always a good one, and when gilt composition runs riot in ferns and fantastic flames, as we frequently see it do around mirrors, its effect is barbaric, rather than elegant.

Broad flats in gilt plaster are less excellent than gold laid on the wood itself.

For prints, where economy has to be much considered, few frames are better than those of flat oak with a bevelled edge, and on the flat a slight design of graceful lines made with the parting-tool, and only the lines gilt. .

Pictures, if small and numerous, should not be dotted about the walls, but grouped. One sometimes see walls as spotted as a currant-dumpling. A band of wood, called a grazing line, behind the chair-backs protects the wall, and is an aid to picture hanging, by giving a line from which we may measure their bases.

If there are many large pictures, they should be hung from a rod placed near the ceiling, or a foot lower, if an ornamental band of paper is carried

round the top of the room below the cornice. If
the cornice is not already "picked out," as the
decorators term it, in colour—that is, delicately
tinted in distemper—it should be done, as it is a
great improvement.

It is not difficult to do this for one's self. The
necessary materials are a pennyworth of whitening,
a pennyworth of size, and of the required tints
a pennyworth. Break up some whitening into
saucers, mix it with water until it is of the con-
sistence of thick cream, add a tablespoonful of
melted size to each saucer, shake in about a
teaspoonful of powdered colour to each, and apply
with a badger or hog-hair paintbrush.

Strong colours become pale tints when mixed
with the whitening, and the mixture dries paler
than it is applied. To paint the ground on which
the plaster design is embossed gives a cameo effect
and is elegant, but sometimes it is better to colour
the raised ornaments. Taste must be the guide
here. This quantity of material is sufficient to tint
every cornice in the house. Splashes of the colour
are easily wiped off while the mixture is wet.

Where the family is small, an oval table, like we generally see in France, is the most convenient form ; as the master and mistress sit facing each other at the narrowest part of the oval, where they can communicate freely with each other, and more easily dispense the general hospitality. A table of this shape is lengthened by leaves inserted in the central division ; when quite closed it is a round table.

A dumb-waiter placed at the right hand of the mistress enables much personal waiting to be dispensed with.

If the dining-room be large, it is desirable to have two sideboards, one larger than the other. The breakfast things should adorn (for that is what they really ought to do) the smaller sideboard.

With all the beauty and comparative cheapness of our Worcester and other pottery, we ought, in every family, to possess such a collection of beautiful objects for daily use as should for ever prevent our sighing after the palmy days of Greek art. I was at Sèvres not long ago, and while going over the porcelain factory there, I mentioned that I had been over that at Worcester. "Ah, then, madame," said the official, "we can show you no more ; you have indeed seen all."

And had we no careless and ever-changing servants to shatter our elegant treasures, we might have in daily use objects which would enrich a museum, and train our eyes to a higher perception of beauty ; and we should learn to value our porcelain, not for its rarity, but for its intrinsic merit.

Look at our picturesque coffee and tea pots, our elegant cups, and well-painted bowls. Why should they always be concealed in china closets, or consigned to kitchen-dressers, while our dining-room walls are too often bare and cheerless ?—a few dismal prints, hung too high to be seen or easily dusted, being frequently the only adornments of a darkened room, like a waiting-room at a railway station for emptiness of anything to occupy the mind, yet which ought to be one of the pleasantest and brightest in the house. Instead of which cheerful appearance, here is a sketch of a regulation dining-room in one of London's broadest brown streets : a room always dark in winter, but in summer exposed to glaring sun and a plague of flies.

As soon as a window is opened to cool the stifling air, a simoom of dust rushes in from the road, and from the dust carts heavily moving to the slow music of the " Trovatore's " *Miserere*, adding a bass to the noise of cabs whirling by to the waltz tunes of " Daughter Angot " and " La belle Hélène."

Tables, chairs, and sideboard are remarkable for nothing but representing so many tons of mahogany embellished with the grinning heads of griffins. Curtains powerfully scented with dust, a large chimney-glass made over to the flies, a heavy bronze machine with ponderous weights and pulleys, all smelling very strongly of gas, chiefly useful for casting deep shadows upon the dining-table. The bean-green carpet, monotonizing with the pea-green walls, whereon hang divers prints of subjects undiscoverable, because they are skied as high as the ceiling will allow, and two " old masters," as two oil paintings are called; one a bitumen-brown Wouvermans, or somebody else, with the hind leg of a gray horse in the foreground, and in the sky a patch of cloud caught in a tree. The other "gem" had been bought at a sale under the impression that its subject was "Angels adoring the Infant Saviour," but which on closer investigation turned out to be two wicked old drunkards playing at cards, purporting to be by a Dutch master.

Could even Giulio Romano's artistic festival have been enjoyed in such a room as this, which is only a fair specimen of the modern British banquet hall? Hear a short extract from Benvenuto Cellini's description of it. After speaking of the rich dress of all the guests and the beauty of the ladies, he continues: "When they had taken their seats, every man produced a sonnet on some subject or other"—for they were a company of poets and artists—"and Michelagnolo read them aloud in a manner which infinitely increased the effect of their excellence. The company fell into discourse, and many fine things were said, and dinner was served up. Behind our backs there were rows of flower-pots, filled with beautiful jessamines, which seemed to heighten the charms of the young ladies beyond expression. Thus we all, with great cheerfulness, began to regale ourselves at that elegant dinner. After our repast was over we were entertained with a concert of music, both vocal and instrumental, and an *improvisatore* recited some admirable verses in praise of the ladies."

We could only on very rare occasions have rows of pots of jasmine placed behind our chairs, but we might easily grow an elder plant to keep off the flies. The Swiss scarlet-berried elder (*Sambucus rufus*) is graceful in growth, and will endure some hard usage.

Flower-pots may also be allowed to remain on the table, unless the plants are cherished pets, and then they will be placed where they can receive the sun and air.

Plants growing outside the windows, especially climbers wreathing the window-frames, give an appearance of size to rooms by bringing air into the perspective. The picturesque effect of the

forms of foliage relieved against the paler sky
is very pleasing, and it breaks the stiff straight
lines of the window better than any drapery.

The glory of the dining-room is its large sideboard. This, where there is a second sideboard,
may be either in the same style or in complete
contrast to it. Here the larger pieces of earthenware and porcelain should be displayed to advantage. These are such things as salad bowls and
outside pie-dishes, which may always remain in the
dining-room, and the whole of the dessert-service,
with the ornaments and table decorations.

The glasses and decanters should always be
elegant, and although in my opinion the Venetian
glass is by far the most beautiful kind, still our
own crystal and engraved glass is often exquisitely
lovely, and the sunshine playing through the pris-
matic decanter knobs, and other cut glass ornaments, gives an unrivalled lustre to the summer
dinner-table. Breakages under careful, delicate
handling would be less frequent than they are
now, so that the expense of procuring glass and
porcelain the best of their kind would not be felt
to be the extravagance it is now.

It will be said that for all this display of glass and china an enormous sideboard will be required, at as enormous a cost. And the first objection I concede, without, however, admitting it to be a fault.

Why should not the sideboard be, if necessary, as large as the side of the room? But the cost may be less than that of an ordinary dinner-waggon. It might be constructed as a series of shelves, ranged as high as can be conveniently reached, broken by cellarettes and other cupboards or cabinets, hung with worked curtains, the shelves merely backed by paper made like embossed leather. There is an infinite variety of styles and forms in which the sideboard may be made; from the gorgeous mass of carved oak and velvet, set with golden shields, and cups, and services of gold plate, such as I have admired on the dining-room walls of a palace built on the ruins of an abbey, down to the stained deal dresser-shaped sideboard of a house of fifty pounds a year, where it would only be decked with graceful, yet unpretending, china and terra-cotta, where its curtains would be of brown holland worked in crewels, and its intrinsic ornaments the burnished brass locks, hinges, and handles. Yet as fine taste might be visible in one as in the other.

The table-cloth, table-napkins, and spoons and forks should be laid in drawers, as such seems their befitting place ; and salt-cellars, and other diminutive articles containing condiments, may be put away behind small curtains, or veils, of decorative needlework, to shelter them from the dust, as well as to give an opportunity for the display of rich and elegant furniture embroidery, adapted in style to the carvings, plaques, inlaid work, or other adornments of the sideboard.

The piles of plates—as many of them must almost of necessity be in piles—will be also concealed and protected by curtains, or behind doors turning on pivots, which, where they are available, are far better than hinges.

The quantity of plates wanted for the daily use of the family must be kept in the kitchen, as they will be washed there, and need to be warmed in readiness for dinner ; but dinner and dessert plates that are not used for greasy comestibles will be rinsed in the dining-room, and rearranged at once.

I know some old Bristol china butter boats of such simple but elegant form, that the curves of the nautilus shell are hardly more graceful. Yet these things had been banished to a kitchen dresser until I implored their release ; and now, in the present Bristol china mania, they are pro-moted to a drawing-room table, a place quite as unsuitable as was the kitchen dresser.

Among useful decorations for the sideboard, some of the prettiest I have seen are the Venetian curved bottles for holding oil and vinegar. They are fixed in a glass stand, and as the curved necks of the flask-shaped bottles bend over across each other, by taking up the stand either oil or vinegar may be poured out without spilling the other con-diment, and the flasks require no stoppers, as their curve is sufficient to keep out the dust, though occasionally a glass dolphin is stuck in the mouth of each bottle. This simple yet ingenious con-trivance is far prettier than our somewhat vulgar cruet-stand. Moorish brass salvers add colour and brightness to the sideboard, in families where silver salvers and presentation plate are not matters of course.

A simple style of dinner is more elegant, as well as more healthful, than one more elaborate. Let it vary with each day rather than with every course : the dinner will thus preserve a character of its own, better than where this is frittered away among so many dishes that you cannot remember off what you have dined.

There is a medium between this fidgety *menu* and the monster joints we sometimes burden ourselves with. It requires judgment to take the right line. We need not attempt, in our everyday dinner, to realize Disraeli's ideal of dining: "eating ortolans to the sound of soft music." But we may try to make our dinner an enjoyment as well as a refreshment ; and although our set banquets may be rare, taste and attention will impart to every meal something of the character of a feast.

Stress must be laid on the importance of having every article of food in its due season.

Independently of the hygienic value of the

change of diet so supplied, which is in itself a substitute for many tonic and alterative medicines, attention to this point will give us luxuries when we may reasonably afford them.

Salmon is as nice when it is a shilling a pound as when it is four times that price, and venison is by no means an expensive viand if the market be watched. If we only think of ribs of beef and legs of mutton, we shall only get beef and mutton. But if we take Nature for our guide, we need not deny ourselves the most gratifying and healthful variety. It is essential that we should eat the fresh fruits as they are ripe, and this rule is equally necessary as regards vegetables.

Indeed, in summer we should accustom ourselves to think more of the vegetable food than of meat ; to arrange our dinner in this department primarily, considering what dainty dishes we may concoct of flour and vegetables fried, boiled, and baked, dressed with oil or milk, herbs or spices, incidentally adding the meat—in fact, reversing our usual order of proceedings, where we construct our dinner plan of solid meat, only throwing in vege-

tables or fruit by way of garnish. But what I
wish to dwell on now is not so much the quantity
of vegetable produce we ought to consume, as
the necessity of its seasonableness.

When our cooks, be they noble, gentle, or
simple, have come to study the medicinal properties of plants—how they act upon the different
organs of the body, and so on—they will see how
beautifully they are adapted by the great Provider
to our bodily requirements, according to the weather
and other circumstances, and how often what
grows best in any situation or soil is the aliment
best suited to our own growth in that situation.

If we attended more to this point, our digestions
would have sufficiently varied exercise to keep
them in healthy working order, and we should hear
less about what does or does not agree with people.
It is of more consequence that our digestions
should be permitted to work at regular hours, than
that they should have an over-easy diet. This,
indeed, is absolutely injurious to them.

Persons sometimes feel ill, and whatever they
may happen to have fed upon is loaded with the

responsibility, and that article of diet is cut off for ever from their list, and its hygienic benefit lost to the constitution. The blame is never laid on irregularity, want of air, exercise, or occupation, excitement or perhaps temper, or upon circumstances generally. Either the weather or the food, irrespective of the quantity taken, is charged with every ill.

If we took care to make pictures of our dishes of fruit, they would afford us two delightful sensations instead of one. To do this it is not needful to have heaps of fruits, or pyramids of pines. A plum on a leaf, an orange on a china tile, with a branch of flowers laid across it, make exquisite pictures.

See how we appreciate the form and grace of a single flower in a specimen glass, so that we cannot now endure to see the mass of crushed flowers we used to call a nosegay ; the very word, so descrip- tive of the bundle, being done away with the thing itself. The old nosegay gave us the scent and gay colours of the flowers, but their tender grace had fled. Now they are delightful to their very stems.

Provident housekeepers have so impressed upon our minds the necessity of caring for the future, that we have been taught to make jam of our most delicious fruits, denying ourselves their fresh beauty and fragrance at our tables, while we roast ourselves over preserving pans in the hottest days of July. This, besides being martyrdom, is a work of supererogation, as the fruit is nicer fresh, and to buy it for the sake of keeping it is absurd, as it can but be eaten once. It is a very reasonable practice in the case of persons possessing large fruit-gardens, as much might otherwise be spoiled ; but in our town households it is trouble taken in vain.

We all know the difference it makes to our dinners whether they are served up hot, or only lukewarm ; and this alone gives a sufficient reason why we should insist upon the kitchen being close to the dining-room. Where there is no possibility of making a door of immediate communication, we should try our utmost to get a slide-window between the two rooms, so that the dishes, and indeed the whole paraphernalia that necessarily moves from kitchen to dining-room, may be placed on a slab at the said window on one side, and taken in at the other side.

If two persons are engaged in performing this work, one dishing up and placing on the window slab, and the other putting the things on the dining-table, it will be very expeditious, but it may be quite easily managed by one person. The slide-window, either a sash or a sliding-door, saves much running to and fro.

I will conclude my remarks upon dining-room furniture with a few words about plate.

The bulk of the plate in daily use in the houses of the upper middle-class is electro-silver, and it is very admissible, being strong, durable, and agreeable to use ; and when made in the ordinary fiddle or threaded patterns is useful without being pretentious. But when it expands into Albert patterns, king's patterns, and the like—when, in short, it claims intrinsic value, and pretends to be silver—it becomes vulgar immediately, because it represents a snobbish feeling which is bent on making a show with a sham. We cannot all afford silver plate, though doubtless we should all like it, but all of us wish to have the most agreeable medium with which to eat our food, and for this purpose electro is as good as silver.

It is better, in purchasing, to buy the best quality, as it is so much more durable, and it always looks better.

For dessert knives and forks, those with mother-of-pearl handles are the best; the colour is so pleasant, and they are very easily cleaned.

Should you happen to be the fortunate possessor of old plate, let nothing induce you to do as many weak persons are talked into doing: exchange it for modern patterns.

Modern plate is seldom of even moderately good design. The object of the manufacturer seems to be to crowd upon it as lumpy an embossed ornament as possible, to make it massive, and remind us of so much per ounce. This was not the motive of the old silversmiths, who more frequently engraved than embossed their orna-ments. Most of the old engraved silver is delight-ful, and it is very light.

The Queen-Anne plate, now so keenly sought, is of admirable workmanship and good design, though the edges are rather thin and sharp for comfort in use.

It is worth while having nice electro dish-covers, as the ugly tin ones sometimes seem to have such a very miserable appearance. It will not be necessary to possess many, and they will come to no harm in our elegant kitchen. They may be either hung up or stood on the dresser; the former way is preferable, and rings to suspend them by are easily attached. Dish covers should be warmed before they are put on, as a cold metal cavern chills a leg of mutton almost to the marrow.

Real silver ornaments for the dinner-table are very precious, but failing these, we may make our tables very elegant with Parian, glass, or even wicker ornaments; and the most interesting of any adornments are vases and dishes painted on porcelain by members of the family. I am sorry to see so many small vulgarities introduced in the shops in the way of *menu* holders, and other so-called ornaments.

Grotesque is all very well, but it should show a light, delicate play of fancy ; and things comic are very amusing when they are not vulgar. But the degenerate caricatures we see about now, mark a tendency to flatter the lowest order of taste, which, if followed, will inevitably drag our conversation down with it. These silly table-decorations began with caricatures of the men who carry the sandwich placards up and down the streets, and daily I see them acquiring all the bad style of common burlesques, or of the cheap valentines.

THE DRAWING-ROOM.

THIS section of our subject involves our relations
with society; and here not even our vanity can
make us believe that modern customs are really
improvements.

What chance has any lady of our time of emula-
ting the graceful manner in which Madame
Récamier held her salon, although she may have
as much learning as Madame de Staël?

We are too heavily weighted, our social intercourse is too complicated, too much clogged with ceremony, to move easily ; and where our highest faculties should be allowed full play, we find so much hard work and consequent fatigue, that we look upon every dinner and evening party in the light of an uphill road with a difficult team to drive.

We all know and applaud the French manner of visiting. Receiving friends on a stated day of the week, simply enjoying their society, and exerting the intellectual faculties instead of merely opening the purse for their entertainment.

Why have we so seldom the courage to follow this example?

It is because we fear to show less well to the eyes of our acquaintance if our own habits seem less expensive than theirs. A low purse-pride is at the bottom of it all. Our dress must be costly and perpetually changing, our servants and establishment must be displayed, if we are ourselves smothered beneath their weight.

So we give up our precious daylight to morning calls, as we ridiculously call those visits of ceremony which are paid in the afternoon. These afford us no pleasure, while they are an infliction to the people called upon. Do not most of us know the feeling of relief that we have after paying a round of visits, when, on finding, as the day was fine, the greater number of our friends from home, we return with an empty card-case, and say, with the complacency of self-satisfied persons who have done their duty, "There, that is done and need not be done again for a month." Whereas we are sorry when even our slight acquaintances "regret they cannot accept" our invitations to an evening party, when we might enjoy their company, and they the society of each other, at the same time, and at a reasonable hour for enjoyment.

Our "at homes" are on a radically wrong principle. We crowd our rooms, we insist on late hours and fullest dress, and our pleasure in consequence becomes a toil.

But how agreeable is the easy evening gathering in a cheerful and early lighted drawing-room, where few or many welcome guests drop in, knowing it to be our "at home" day. Where we talk and sip

tea, play and sing, or amuse ourselves, if clever,
with paper games—capital promoters of laughter
and whetstones to the wits—and go away as early
as we please. All to be over by half-past ten, at
any rate, in order not to interfere with early rising
next morning. I have found nothing, not even
guinea lessons from eminent masters, more con-
ducive to family improvement in music than this
way of enjoying society, since one is obliged to
have a few new things always at one's fingers'
ends ready to perform ; and in homely little parties
like these, young girls "not yet out" may pass
many pleasant evenings under their mother's wing,
with real advantage to themselves.

The simpler the dress worn by the ladies who
are "at home," the better the taste shown. Here
again we may learn much from the French, who
perfectly understand the art of *demi-toilette.*

Our theatres and concert-rooms are filled night
after night by people who pay to be entertained.
They never take food in their pockets, and the
passing to and fro of sellers of refreshment is felt
to be a nuisance. Why should people who have

dined late be supposed to want supper, unless they
have been dancing, or are sitting up later than is
good for them? And the proof that they do not
want it is in the very little they take of it, except
some stout elderly ladies who prepared for it before
they came, and who consequently have felt too low
all the evening to be moderately cheerful.

People who dine early always make a solid tea
about six o'clock. It is only the *bourgeois* class
who love their hot suppers, and the taste stamps
them.

How can we use hospitality one towards another
without grudging, when, instead of being able to
rejoice that a friend is sharing our daily pursuits
and repasts, we must spend a fortune in jellies,
pastry, and unwholesome sweets, whenever we
invite our friends inside our doors; when we are
compelled to import from the confectioner piles
of plates, dishes, and hired cutlery, turn our
houses into scenes of confusion for a week, and
feed our children upon what have been aptly called
" brass knockers," the remains of the feast? No
wonder most of us dread giving a party! No; I

would have special banquets on special occasions
—Christmas, comings of age, marriages, silver,
and above all golden, weddings, welcomes from
abroad, and other joyful days. But our enjoyment of society need not be limited to such obser-
vances as these, but rather the crop of friendship
increased by attentive cultivation.

"Has friendship increased?" asks wise Sir
Arthur Helps. "Anxious as I am to show the
uniformity of human life, I should say that this,
one of the greatest soothers of human misery, has
decreased."

Lady Morgan, an experienced leader of society,
used to tell me, "My dear, give them plenty of
wax-candles and people will enjoy themselves ; "
to which I add, manage the music well, and teach
your daughters to help you, and cultivate musical
young men, keeping, however, the law in your own
hands.

Almost the only art we have not spoiled by
machinery is music—for we do not consider the
barrel-organ in the light of music.

Perhaps it is because in this art we had scope

for invention, not finding a good thing ready made to our hands by the Greeks, which we might imitate mechanically, and become slaves of its tradition. Possibly it is a blessing in disguise that the music of the ancients is lost to us, for having no models we have no fetters.

There is, however, in music, less liberty for the performer than for the master-inventor ; and this is as it should be : we interpret his greater mind. Wilful music is seldom pleasing.

What Ruskin says about truth of line in drawing applies equally to music ; In the rapid passages of a *presto* by Beethoven, the audience at St. James's Hall would know if Hallé played one single note out, even if he slightly touched the corner of a wrong black key; for our ears have been wonderfully trained. And the time must be as accurate as the tone, and the proper degree of light and shade must be expressed, or you are no master. What must it be to be the creator of the music which it is so difficult even to copy !

Yet in our drawing-rooms we permit people to talk all the time music is being played, showing

respect neither to the composition nor to the performer. This should not be, and abroad this ill-
bred custom has not obtained.

There is, however, something to be said on the
other side. The music we hear in society is frequently either flimsy and not worth studying ; or
it is too difficult for the capacity of the performer,
perhaps having been learnt in too idle a manner,
in which case conversation shields the composer.

But the chief cause of the distressing rudeness
complained of, is that there is too much music at
a party, and it is not well arranged. Glees are
got up and fail deplorably ; harps and flutes are
not in tune with other instruments ; people accompany songs they have never seen before ; and much
time and talk are consumed in wishing for absent
tenor or bass voices. A little good music would
have been delightful ; the noise of so many imper-
fect efforts is only a bore.

In our parties we carelessly lose Nature's purest
delights : those which appeal most strongly to our
finest perceptions. Is it not true enjoyment to sit
among the roses on a balcony listening to a sweet

voice within singing an air of Schubert or Mozart? And if the charm be enhanced by moonlight, it is a pleasure for the gods!

It is true that roses will not flourish on London balconies, the coal-smoke being so injurious to them; but pinks, and many other fragrant flowers, grow well and easily, without the cost of frequent renewal required for roses. The general use of window gardens, and the due encouragement of greenery over our houses, would tend much to improve our vitiated atmosphere, and we may have the gratification of feeling that we are doing good to our neighbours while we cultivate plants for our own benefit. Perhaps, by-and-by, a tax may be charged upon every empty window-sill.

The front and back of every house would make a good-sized bit of garden, only it will be per-pendicular instead of horizontal. We ought all to grow our own pears trained against the walls, as these ripen as well in town as in the country; and most of us might dwell under our own vines and fig-trees.

A balcony, however small it may be, is an extra

room, and frequently it is a good play-room for
children if kept clean and well syringed. No
training is better for children than the culture
of flowers—it unites work and play with every
advantage of both. It is an education in itself.
Mr. Gladstone calls the love of flowers a peculiarly
English taste. He seems to have forgotten the
special fondness for plants shown by the French
and Belgians; though the Dutch tulip mania
reminds one somewhat of a commercial speculation. His remarks on the children's flower-show
held at Grosvenor House merit particular attention.
He observes that owing to the increased value of
land, large masses of the population are removed
from contact with nature, and at this period it is
important that every family should learn that they
possess a resource in the cultivation of flowers both
in their cottages and windows, and at every point
where contact with the open air may be obtained.
He hopes that with the needful improvements in
the dwellings of the poor, some means may be
devised for fostering cottage horticulture and
cottage floriculture.

Wind and scorching sunshine are the great adversaries to window gardening, but both of these evils may be obviated by simple contrivances in · the way of screens.

Very few plants can be cultivated in our sitting-rooms with advantage either to themselves or to our furniture. They are greatly injured by gas, as well as by the dry heat of our fires, while they cause a dampness in the atmosphere which speedily produces mildew and other ill effects of moisture.

We should bear in mind, in furnishing a drawing-room, that the guests are the principal part of the furniture, and leave sufficient space for the number we wish our room to hold. A drawing-room as empty as one of Orchardson's pictures may be overcrowded by twenty people.

The walls may be adorned to profusion with objects of taste, without their inconveniently occupying space ; but tiny tables and flower-pot stands are often in jeopardy.

In a room crowded with furniture the guests cannot circulate—one because there is not space enough to pass between a lady's' dress and the

small table with a vase upon it that is so likely
to be upset; another because an ottoman just
before her keeps her a prisoner on the sofa where
she was planted on entering the .room—until
ladies are thankful to do a little something in-
audible at the piano as a pretext for moving, and
gentlemen are only too glad to be required to force
a passage in the service of a lady. And this not
merely in the absurd and terrible crush at an
"at home" in the London season, but at a simple
evening party anywhere.

It is often agreeable to have several afternoon
tea-tables in the drawing-room, as the ladies can
pair off at each, and become pleasantly acquainted
while serving each other. But in the case of large
musical "at homes," it is better to have refresh-
ments served in the dining-room, as the clatter
of spoons and the bustle of waiting disturbs the
music; besides injury being often done by ice
plates left about, tea spilt, and crumbs trodden
into the carpet.

We will now leave the subject of parties and
study the drawing-room in its ordinary appearance

as the sitting-room of the family out of working hours. A drawing-room should be used, and look as if it were used, and if used properly it need never be dirty nor in disorder. A library, or study, greatly aids the drawing-room by preventing its too indiscriminate use. Indeed, where boys and girls have school-work to prepare, this is almost a matter of necessity, as there is neither rest nor comfort for their elders while lessons are going on; and if other members of the family occupy themselves much in writing or painting, it is a great hindrance to have to remove their paraphernalia every time the table is required for some other purpose.

The room may be called a study, morning-room, or library, according to its purpose, bearing in mind that although the name is more high sounding, a library with few books is only ridiculous. And when there are many and good books, the room must be held in great respect, and those who use it trained to extreme neatness and order. I find it a good plan to instal my eldest son as responsible librarian at a small salary; he sees that the younger children put away their books after them.

A gas-standard lights a study better than anything else for general use, though "the Queen's reading lamp" is good for weak eyes.

The standard must be firm on its base, so as not easily to upset; it is less in the way if it stands on the floor rather than on the table, and it should be capable of being raised to the height of six feet, or lowered to any point. It ought to be easily movable in any direction, and the tube long enough to admit of its being placed in any part of the room. The only kind of tubing that really prevents a disagreeable smell escaping from the gas is the snake tubing. I had at first a kind that was dearer than the ordinary india-rubber tubing, but, although assured by the gasfitter that it would be inodorous, I was obliged to change it for the snake, for which I paid twelve shillings, and have had no trouble since.

We all know that wax candles are the nicest and most becoming light for a drawing-room ; but they are dear, and candlesticks, however elegant, require frequent cleaning. The commoner kind of candles are greasy, and grease is very troublesome when it drops about, though wax and sperm are readily removed by warming the spots. There is a kind of candle called the dropless candle which answers very well to its name.

Paraffin, and almost all patent candles, fill the air with burnt smoke, and this, to many people, is insufferable.

Sperm candles are preferable to any others for general use at the piano and for bed-rooms. And candles need not be an expensive item when a house is well fitted with gas, as much music practising may be done by daylight and gaslight; while in bed-rooms we ought not to require much length of candlelight.

There is no need of more than one candle to be carried about, and that is for the person who turns off the gas to go upstairs with.

An Italian *lucerna* is a picturesque object for this purpose ; oil is burnt in it—colza will do, though they burn olive oil in Italy, and it gives double the light of colza. On no account use petroleum, or any of the mineral oils. Besides their horrible smell and associations, all the kinds are more or less explosive, and for the little use for which we should require lamps, the difference in cost is trifling.

One occasionally sees curious and quaint old iron or bronze candlesticks, and it is well to seize the opportunity of purchasing such treasures ; but if not fortunate enough to get a better thing, it is easy to procure one of those funny little brass candlesticks, in the shape of a frying-pan, so commonly used in the Belgian hotels.

As there are no servants in our model establishment, tallow candles need never be bought, and no candlebox will be required, nor any kitchen candlesticks, to be stuck periodically in a row in the fender to melt their grease and solder, and lose their extinguishers and snuffers.

So we see, even in this small instance, how a young couple beginning to furnish will want few of these superfluities, and, not being compelled to buy common things for servants, may afford things of choice quality for themselves, and to these they may add others as time goes on.

Take, for another example, the breakfast-cups ; they may at first buy two very pretty cups and saucers for their own use, and a third equally pretty for their lady friend, or help, as they may like to call her; and either title is honourable, only one seems kinder than the other.

And so they need not purchase what is called a whole set, or, more shopmanly, a "suite," comprising a dozen of almost everything, whose chief merit is in its completeness, of which we tire ; and this merit is destroyed when on breaking one of the two bread-and-butter plates we find it is a last year's pattern, and cannot be matched at the shop without its being specially made for us.

How much more we should be attached to a pretty thing if we could say of it : "Don't you remember we bought that cup when So-and-So came to stay with us ? " Such associations endow everyday objects with life.

The original outlay throughout the house may proceed in like manner, and spare rooms may be furnished after the other rooms.

This would enable more young people to marry,

and they need not go to a shop whose advertisements recommend them to furnish on the three
years' system, by the end of which time they will
have paid double the value of their furniture, and
most of it will probably be discarded, or broken in
pieces.

Perhaps a day may come when nobody will heed
an advertisement, and only look at a circular when
they write memoranda on its clean side. Then our
postmen will be spared the bulk of their work,
which makes it a perpetual Valentine's-day for
them.

It is too visionary to hope that our eyes may
cease to be distressed by posters blazing everywhere, or that nearly half of every book or
newspaper we buy may not be made up of
advertisements.

But no more on this irritating topic, as I would
only counsel those about to furnish not to be too
much tempted with novelties, especially patent
novelties.

Some of us are beginning to tire of the medi-
ævalism which was the natural reaction from the

preposterous designs of the wall-papers, curtains, and other furniture which disguised our rooms— the ridiculous carpets with such patterns as orange-blossoms tied with white satin favours ("So sweet for a bride"), and rugs with huge blue roses.

But we have now gone too far the other way, and made all our houses like "High" churches, not permitting even the simplest unconventional design to interfere with the severity of our Gothic taste. This is a mistake; for as our houses ought not to be turned into Greek temples, as they were in the time of the first French Empire, as little should they be decorated like Gothic churches.

Many styles, and many beautiful yet diverse objects, may be made to harmonize by tasteful arrangement; and this freer latitude is well adapted to our varied moods and our many-sided lives. Few people of moderate means can carry out one style in its entirety.

I have seen a very handsome drawing-room fitted up perfectly in the Louis Quatorze style, and spoiled by some German bead-mats on the table;

L

and some of the most beautiful upholstery I ever saw, of Neo-Greek designs painted on straw-coloured satin, covering chairs of purely Greek form, looked droll on a Brussels carpet with fuchsias upon it.

Twenty years ago, people of taste and pretension to archæological knowledge furnished their houses in the Elizabethan style, with the result of uncomfortable furniture abounding in anachronisms.

The Queen Anne style, so fashionable at present, is far better suited to modern requirements than is the Elizabethan, which is of necessity kept exclusively English. The Jacobean style too is less rigid, as we may with propriety consider that much French and Italian elegance had been imported into the court of Scotland by the two French queens and Mary Stuart. The possession of a portrait by Vandyke would be of itself enough to make one wish to furnish a house in the stately and elegant style of his time.

Although it may not be so pure in taste, the style of the Renaissance is eminently adapted for comfortable household service. The delicate arabesques

and grotesques followed from Raffaelle's adornments of the Vatican are not too precious for use
in household decoration—where painting cannot be
expected to last as long as pictures framed and
out of reach of daily handling—and yet they are
graceful enough to refresh without exciting a tired
mind.

Any one possessing artistic taste and some training can work out these fanciful decorations for
home gratification, and being cherished, they will
last three or four times as long as the graining of
the house-painter. Besides, and this is a great
consideration in cities, all the majolica ornaments
and tiles, which are so suitable to this style of
decoration, will wash, and be bright and clear for
ever. Do not despise the Renaissance, for there is
much delight in it, though not of the highest kind.
We may keep the higher things for higher uses.

A Brussels carpet of Persian pattern is very nice
for a drawing-room, as it is unobtrusive, and yet
it is cheerful, and suits most styles of furniture.
This, like the dining-room carpet, had better be
made with a border, and so as to allow of a margin

of the floor round it being varnished. If edged with fringe its appearance is enriched ; and I do not in practice find the fringe inconveniently displaced by ladies' dresses, nor in dusting, as I feared it might be when I added it to a carpet which required enlarging.

The remarks on dining-room curtains and rods apply equally here, as it is of great consequence that the room should be easily cleaned.

For a young couple beginning to furnish, it may be well to have some of the pretty *cretonnes* for curtains and chair-coverings, which would last clean and bright while better were being worked on simple materials from patterns, either original or borrowed from the Art Needlework Society. Then the *cretonne* curtains might be hung in the newly furnished spare bed-room. ' The chair-coverings would be replaced one by one as others were worked or nice materials met with.

In doing fancy-work, it is better to make one good thing large enough to take a pride in, than countless little elegances, such as mats, antimacassars, table banner-screens, etc., which seldom last

long, and are terribly in the way. The time consumed in making pincushions, pocket-tidies, and
tiny knick-knacks, would serve to tapestry a room,
let alone making curtains for it.

Where there are fine views from the windows,
they are better framed as pictures than curtained.
Draperies, if they are very beautiful, are more
favourably displayed when facing the light (as in
the case of *portières*) than at the windows, where
they are liable to fade, and the light shining
through them hides their beauty. Draught more
often enters from doorways than by the windows ;
and in summer doors are often unhung for the
sake of coolness and additional space, and the
portières are comfortable to use on chilly days.

Venetian blinds are the best of any interior
blinds, though window awnings are much pleasanter in summer. Red tammy enriches the colour
of the room, but it is not agreeable to sit long in
a room filled with the flame-coloured light, though
this softens as the blinds fade, which they soon do.
Yellow blinds are very disagreeable, and tryingly
sunny in summer. Blue are as unpleasantly cold, and

make people look like ghosts. White holland gives as soft a light as any, and if carefully used the blinds will not go awry. Green tammy is good, but it soon fades.

With a gas fire there is no occasion for a hearth-rug, though fur and other large rugs look very comfortable spread before the windows in winter, and Indian mats look cool in summer, and preserve the carpet from fading.

In buying furniture it is safer to move cautiously. Seize, by all means, anything that strikes you as being "just the very thing," the moment you see it, or it may escape you for ever ; but do not be beguiled into buying a whole "suite" of everything at once, because you think you may as well finish the work while you are about it, but let your taste, as well as wisdom, have time to grow. We all know the feeling of vexation we endure when we have committed ourselves to any particular thing, and find subsequently something which would have suited us very much better.

Whatever you buy or make, do not let it be rubbish. Things ill considered get dreadfully in

our way, and by-and-by we cannot endure their
discordance; that is, if they last long enough for
us to weary of them. When you purchase anything, remember that it has to be taken care of
and dusted every day, and the smaller the trifle
the more troublesome it is to keep clean. Think,
before you buy it, whether or not you will like it
when it is tarnished, and if you can value it sufficiently to devote thought and a minute of time to
it every day for years.

We squander our money on frippery—not in
dress merely, but in hideous ornaments for our
fire-places, in antimacassars of disagreeably sug-
gestive name, in toys and trinkets and imitation
rubbish of all kinds, which encumber our table-
surfaces, and are dust-traps occupying the minds
and mornings of our parlour-maids to keep them
clean. We spend in this taste-destroying trash the
change of the twenty pounds which would have
bought one ornament of real beauty, which would
only take the same time to dust as one of the fifty
frivolities costing from half-a-crown to seven-and-
sixpence each.

This is mostly so much waste, or worse, because it helps the habit of foolish, ill-considered spending ; and while we thus bedizen our drawing-rooms, we render them so uninhabitable that they fall out of use for our own comfort, and become merely show places for visitors.

A long article might be written on dusting. We can hardly have too little of the carpet-broom (which all housemaids love to use every week to the detriment of our carpets), and hardly too much of the feather-brush for lightly touching curtains, walls, and pictures, or of the duster for rubbing furniture. If a little is done daily, furniture will never need polishing, but will always look bright, as dust will not have entered the crevices.

It is easier, and also better for the durability of carpets, to take them up occasionally to be beaten, and have the dusty floor beneath them cleaned, than to have everything smothered weekly in the dust raised by the carpet-broom. A pair of steps is necessary in a house where cleanliness is attended to, to unhang curtains and pictures and replace them after dusting. The walls need to be whisked over weekly with the feather-brush.

The elegant china and glass gaseliers which are now so general are easily cleaned with a damp sponge; those of Venetian glass are still more beautiful, and not much more expensive : these also can be washed with little trouble. Adopting the plan of cleaning one room each day, it will not take a great deal of time, or cause much fatigue; while the light daily dusting required is a mere nothing to any one doing it dexterously.

I have a great dislike of chiffoniers; the very name presupposes them receptacles of *chiffons* and lumber. I cannot see any use for them in a drawing-room. Music-books should be in the music-stand, a lady's work in her work-table, and books either in use or put away in the book-case.

A portfolio-stand is of great service in preserving and displaying drawings and prints which require careful and practised handling. Sir Felix Slade, the eminent print-collector, used to complain that many persons, especially young ladies, made a bent mark with their thumbs in the margin of an engraving; he always insisted on having his prints taken up by what he called their north-west corner, and carefully laid on the print-stand. A portfolio-stand should have a piece of stuff laid over the books and cases, wrapped inside the woodwork of the stand. This is easily removed when the stand is in use; as it is left hanging down on one side, it keeps much dust from the pictures, and if of some nice silk or other stuff is ornamental in itself.

A sofa with a rack-end to let down at pleasure at any angle is a great convenience, but such couches are not often made, unless especially ordered.

Numerous mirrors injure the repose of a room, causing bewilderment; but one or two are pleasing, as they have the effect of water in a landscape, repeating the lines and echoing the forms of objects. They also tend to give space, though not to the same extent as pictures do, which are the most decorative of all ornaments; and when they are very good they rank with our most precious possessions.

Brackets may be appropriately used for ornaments, such as terra-cotta and others; a few fine bronzes, besides being handsome in themselves, give value to the colouring of a room.

BED AND DRESSING ROOMS.

Ventilation — Window curtains and blinds — Bedsteads — Spring mattresses — Towels — Danger of fire at the toilet — Mantelpiece — Pictures and frames — Superfluous necessaries — Taine's criticisms — Aids to reading in bed — Service of the bath — Improvements in washstands — Arranging the rooms — Attics made beautiful — Sick-rooms — Neatness — Disinfectants — Chlorine gas — Condy's solution — Filters — Invalid chairs — Generous efforts of the medical profession to improve the national health.

WE pass a third of our time in our bed-rooms when we are in health, and the whole of it when we are ill ; therefore their ventilation and general arrangement demand our most earnest consideration.

Some bed-rooms are draughty, occasioning cold and neuralgia, but the more common fault is that they are not airy enough ; for with our extreme attention to what is called " English comfort," we too frequently make our bed-rooms almost air-tight.

This causes restlessness by night and headache by day. It were far better to accustom ourselves to sleep with our windows open, as the night air is not at all injurious in dry weather, unless an east wind is blowing. We must be guided by the weather, and trim to the wind; our feeling will tell us whether we may, or may not, safely leave our windows open much more surely than the almanac. The time when windows should be shut throughout the house is when the dew is rising and falling; then the damp enters and saturates everything.

People seldom attend to this point, but keep their windows open too late in the afternoon, which in Italy is recognized as the dangerous time. We have but little malaria in England, but what little there is is at work just before and after sun-set. Many persons, too, who like myself have immense faith in fresh air, throw open their windows on leaving their rooms in the morning, regardless of whether the air be dry and warm, or whether a fog or bitter east wind will penetrate the whole house to damp or chill it. It is more prudent, in case of bleak or raw weather, to wait for an hour or two before opening the windows, ventilation from the door being sufficient for the room while it is empty.

It is useless to lay down laws as to the windows in our variable climate. We must work by our natural thermometer, and let our skin perform one of its most useful functions and tell us whether it is cold or hot ; but if our feelings are uncertain, give judgment in favour of fresh air.

If your rooms have the old-fashioned long and narrow windows which are always found in houses built in the reigns of the early Georges, the Japanese paper curtains, being very cheap, are as good as any, the intention being to drape a skeleton window, which curtainless is a dismal object.

But more modern windows should not, or at least need not, have long hanging curtains, but only just sufficient to cover the window without leaving a streak of light. The drapery may hang

from one side or from both, according to taste;
but unless you are very particular to admit no
light in your bed-room, a mere valance, or some
ornament at the top of the window, is enough.
For instance, some pretty design in fretwork, as
the tracery of an Arabian arch, made of deal
an inch thick, cut out with a steam saw and
stained or enamelled black, would be effective
when lined with rose colour, or any drapery suited
to your room ; and you might furnish an appropriate design for the fretwork. This would be
easily dusted, and is not expensive.

White blinds are clean and pleasant for bed-
rooms, but dark-green ones are better for persons
with weak sight; either these or Venetian blinds
are very useful where there are no shutters.

Brass and iron bedsteads have almost entirely
superseded wooden ones, and they are generally
made without fittings for curtains. Indeed, in our
well-built modern houses there are so few draughts
to be guarded against that curtains are seldom
necessary.

In bed-rooms of the present time valances to the

beds are quite superfluous, as the bed-round is completely out of fashion. This was the name of the breadth of carpet which went round three sides of the bed, leaving the remainder of the floor bare. The fashion was healthy and economical, certainly, but it was tryingly ugly and cheerless.

For a bed-room, nothing is so good as the square carpet, with a broad margin of the floor stained and varnished, as this is very easily taken up for the floor and carpet to be cleaned. The carpet must be laid down the first time by a man from the carpet-warehouse, so that it may be evenly stretched, which is seldom done by a carpenter; but after that it is easily spread, as it remains in shape, and needs very few nails to keep it in position.

Bed-room carpets need not have brown paper laid under them, though this is an advantage in other rooms, as it keeps dust and draught from coming through the cracks of the floor, besides saving the carpet from being cut by the edges of the boards. Kidderminster carpets are now made in very nice patterns, and are quite suitable for bed-rooms where Brussels carpets may be thought too expensive.

A hearth-rug is more useful in a bed-room than elsewhere, as a bed-room fire should be of coal or wood, and not of gas, as this is injurious in a bed-room.

Take care never to let the head of the bed be placed before the fire-place. This is sometimes foolishly done, and unsuspecting sleepers get neuralgia from it. In summer a pretty pattern, cut out in tissue-paper so as to resemble lace, tacked on a slight frame covered with black tarletane, and fitted into the fire-place, allows ventilation and keeps out the dust from the chimney. Little girls love to cut these fire-papers, and one of them, with care, lasts two summers, and often three.

When there are no bed-curtains, it is sometimes advisable to line the ironwork at the head of the bed, so that the sleeper may not be exposed to draught. Spring mattresses, with soft woollen mattresses upon them, are the most comfortable beds of any ; and Heal's folding spring mattresses,

though expensive, cannot be too strongly recommended. These spring beds are so easily made
up, that this is a matter of very trifling consideration in any house where there are two pairs of
hands, children's or grown-up people's. It is
necessary to turn back the bed-clothes completely
over the foot of the bed, and leave it to air for
an hour, at least, after the window has been
opened. There is a great fancy now for having
trimmed pillow-covers, and pieces of ornamental
needlework to spread over the bed after it is
turned down; the fashion is pretty, but superfluous, as a nicely worked counterpane looks
equally well, and need nòt be folded up at bed-
time.

Towels may, and should be, ornamented, but not
so much as to make them inconvenient for use.
The collection of linen exhibited by the Duchess
of Edinburgh gave many of us an interesting
lesson in things of this kind. One of the silliest
pieces of finery seen in a bed or dressing room is
the trimmed towel-horse cover. Towels cannot
possibly dry if the evaporation is stopped, and

M

even when the cover is made of thin muslin, it is only a troublesome frivolity.

Every lady has her own particular taste about her toilet-table, so that I only give a caution to let it be safe, and not liable to take fire. We frequently want candles on our dressing-tables; therefore it stands to reason that the veil often placed over the looking-glass is highly dangerous. This drapery is intended to keep the sun from scorching the back of the glass, but it is safer to stand the glass elsewhere than in the window when the room is exposed to the midday sun, although it will not be so pleasant for use.

The rose-lined white muslin petticoat which was once such a popular way of concealing a deal dressing-table is highly dangerous. Indeed, it is difficult to conceive any combination more inflammable than the veiled glass set in the midst of cotton window-curtains, and two candles standing on a cotton toilet-cover, with a frilled muslin pincushion between them, and full muslin drapery below.

The most convenient table allows the large

square-seated stool, so comfortable to sit on while
dressing the hair, to be pushed under it when not
in use. When light ornaments are placed on a
bed-room mantelpiece and exposed to a current
of air, it is advisable to have two upright pieces
of board, painted, cut out, or otherwise made
ornamental, placed one on each side of the shelf
to protect the knick-knacks from being blown
down ; and if these are numerous, one or two
shelves may be put above the mantelpiece, forming a pretty little museum of curiosities which
may be too small, or too trifling, to be placed
with advantage in the drawing-room ; and houses
of the class I am describing seldom have a
boudoir. If the mantelpiece is covered with
cloth or velvet, the shelves and back might be
covered with the same, and this would be very
becoming to the ornaments. Tunisian or point
lace forms a very good edging to a mantelboard,
and when a foot deep, or nearly so, it is extremely
handsome. Water-colour sketches should abound
in a bed-room, souvenirs of places we have visited,
or of friends who have made the drawings, being

doubly enjoyed when we are recovering from illness, or when we are awake early in the summer morning. Sketches are as pleasant as books, without the trouble of holding them up to our eyes. They should be carefully arranged so as not to look spotty; and they must be hung flat against the wall by having the rings placed high in the frames, as, although it is becoming to the pictures, the effect of them hanging much forward makes many people giddy, and in an invalid will sometimes produce a feeling akin to sea-sickness.

Neatly made frames of the cheap German gilding (which will wash) answer very well for sketches hung in the less prominent situations in a bedroom, and bring a luxury within the reach of many who would not otherwise afford it.

Now I am come to the difficult part of my subject—the tug of war, in fact—for I want men to do something for themselves, and women to do without something dear to their hearts. I think I will speak of the latter clause first.

In bed-rooms especially is seen that truly English love of superfluous comforts which we mistake for civilization : it meets us everywhere, in and out of the house, but it abounds in our bed and dressing rooms.

The amount of toilet so-called necessaries is incredible, and the number of patent objects over-whelming. When we consider that seven things only are necessary to our personal neatness and cleanliness—soap, sponge, towel, and tooth-brush for washing, and brush and comb and nail-scissors for the rest of the toilet—and then count the other paraphernalia seen in our dressing-rooms, we shall discover how many frivolous trades our superfluities maintain, to say nothing of ingenuity misplaced in making advertisements of dressing-cases and hair-restorers conspicuously attractive.

The toilet-table is not alone to blame : the fault pervades the whole house and overwhelms the bed-rooms.

M. Taine, in his "Notes on England," amusingly describing an English house, says, "In my bed-room is a table of rosewood, standing on an oil-cloth mat on the carpet ; upon this table is a slab of marble, on the marble a round straw mat—all this to bear an ornamented water-bottle covered with a tumbler. One does not simply place one's book on a table: upon the table is a small stand for holding it. One does not have a plain candle-stick : the candle is enclosed in a glass cylinder, and is furnished with a self-acting extinguisher. All this apparatus hampers ; it involves too much trouble for the sake of comfort."

This was only a bachelor's room ; what would the French critic have thought of the aids to reading in bed in an ordinarily well-appointed bed-room where the master indulges in that practice ?

By the Englishman's bedside is also a small table standing on a mat, and on this table another mat supporting a patent stand which screws up and down, and on this another mat with a candlestick with a nozzle and a patent protector of the candle from the draught, a glass shield set in an ormolu frame which has an elaborate screw ; and by the side of the candlestick-stand another mat, on which is a patent screw for shading the light from the aforesaid candle. Then, besides the extinguisher, also on a stand and a mat, and patent matches in a patent box, he is supplied with a book-rest which will turn in every possible way, with a patent leaf-turner and leaf-holder, and a variety of other little conveniences. He only lacks an electric communication between the fire-escape outside and the patent night-bolt on his door, to prevent him being burnt in his bed, to make the thing complete.

We feel how difficult we have made life by having to put all these indispensables to their intended use. We have multiplied these patent gimcracks until we cannot move without being crushed by our comforts; and the keeping of all this in order obliges us to have under us a parlour-maid, an upper housemaid, and an under house-maid, to wait upon these inventions. Helps, in one of his essays, says, " I have always maintained that half the work of the world is useless, if subjected to severe scrutiny. My idea of organization would be to diminish much of this useless work." The same remark applies to our luggage when we travel. We take things fancying. We may want them, forgetting that it is easier to do without an article once, than to have the trouble of packing it and looking after it every day ; so we bury our pleasure under a heap of care.

I must give another extract from Taine's description of his bed-room before I proceed to my second great battle-field, where I fear a harder contest.

After describing his dressing-table, Taine goes on to say of his washstand : " It is furnished with one large jug, one small one, a medium one for hot water, two porcelain basins, a dish for tooth-brushes, two soap-dishes, a water-bottle with its tumbler, a finger-glass with its glass. Underneath is a very low table, a sponge, another basin, a large shallow zinc bath for morning bathing. In a cup-board is a towel-horse with four towels of different kinds, one of them thick and rough. Napkins are under all the vessels and utensils ; to provide for such a service, when the house is occupied, it is necessary that washing should be always going on. The servant comes four times a day into the rooms : in the morning to draw the blinds and the curtains, open the inner blinds, carry off the boots and clothes, and bring a large can of hot water with a fluffy towel on which to place the feet; at midday and at seven in the evening to bring water and the rest, in order that the visitor may wash before luncheon and dinner; at night to shut the window, arrange the bed, get the bath ready, renew the linen ;—all this with silence, gravity, and respect. Pardon these trifling details, but they must be handled in order to figure to one's self the wants of an Englishman in the direction of his luxury: what he expends in being waited upon and comfort is enormous, and one may laughingly say that he spends the fifth of his life in his tub."

Men will do much for glory and for vainglory, even to using cold shower-baths in winter, and boast of breaking the ice in them ; but I never yet heard of a man who would take the trouble to empty his bath after using it. Now I maintain that every man who has not a valet ought to do this. Few men consider the hard work it is to a woman to carry upstairs heavy cans of water; but that is trifling, compared with the difficulty to a woman of turning the water out of a large flat bath into a pail. A man would find little difficulty in doing this; his arms are longer, his back stronger, and his dress does not come in the way.

When a man likes to have his bath regularly—and who does not?—he should think of the labour that half a dozen or more baths entail, and in the evening prepare his can of water for to-morrow's use, place his own bath on his piece of oil-cloth, enjoy his tub to his heart's content, pour away the water, put up his tub, and say nothing about it.

This disagreeable lecture over, we will go on and see how easy the general dressing-room arrangements might be made.

If, instead of our ordinary washstands with their jugs and basins, we had fixed basins with plugs in them and taps above, much of the water-bearing difficulty would be obviated. These washstands should be placed back to back, as it were, in every two rooms, having only the partition-wall between them, so that the same pipe would supply two taps.

I have three sorts of basins in use in my house:

one kind has the ordinary tap and plug, another kind has handles for supply and waste, the water being sucked away on turning the waste handle. This is safe for careless people who let rings or any other articles drop in the basin, and nothing but water can go down to choke the pipe. But the basin I find easiest and most pleasant to use, tilts out the water by lifting a handle, or rather finger-niche, in front of the basin ; and when this is let fall it strikes on an india-rubber pad beneath the tap, so that the basin cannot be cracked. All these different basins are fitted into marble washstands with dishes for soap and tooth-brushes hollowed in the marble, with holes for drainage connected with the waste-pipe below. These conveniences, with a housemaid's-closet with sink and tap on the same floor, save all carrying up and down of pails and cans of water, and, in fact, the heaviest part of a housemaid's work.

Where the hall is warmed by hot-water pipes, water from the same source will supply the bed-rooms. It will be warm if the first quart is allowed to flow away. Or the pipes may be connected with the kitchen boiler, which, in the case of our kitchen on the ground floor, will not be so expensive as where the pipes have to communicate with the basement.

Supplying the taps is perfectly easy when only cold water is required, and children and delicate persons may be indulged with jugs of warm water, which, however, every boy using should fetch for himself. We should thus be able to dispense with ewers and toilet-cans, which would at once pay for the fitting of the pipe and tap to each room.

It is better and nicer to use filtered water for the toilet-decanter, and not water drawn directly from the cistern, unless it has been tested and found pure. In such a case, which is rare, no decanter will be needed, unless we like to have a Venetian glass one for the sake of its beauty.

Let all persons, in dressing, replace the things they have used, and spread their towels on the horse to dry ; then the rooms will be set in order for the day, only needing the daily dusting, which will be done after the beds are made. Boys and girls who go to school should make their beds before they go, so they must open them to air immediately they get up.

" These seem little things : and so they are unless you neglect them " (*Sir A. Helps*).

Everybody should have his or her own wardrobe, and keep it in order.   Men and boys and little children will have everything neatly made and mended for them, and laid in its proper place ; so all they have to do is to leave the drawers as tidy as they found them, taking heed not to lose their gloves and neckties ; the larger things take care of themselves.   The secret of keeping one's clothes tidy is not to have too many.

Of course, where there are no servants to provide for, the house has fewer rooms than a family of the same size requires in our present experience, and the uglier part of the house is abolished, or where not abolished, is converted from servants' bed-rooms and attics—unpleasant, dusty, and ill furnished ; redolent of tallow candle, shoes, brushes, and stale perfumery ; with closed windows and the floor strewn with old letters, hair-pins, half-empty match-boxes, and dogs-eared penny novels—into a bowerlike study or morning-room, where a young lady may entertain herself and her own especial visitors. I have even known an attic in Baker Street so converted by the invention and taste of a young lady, as to live in one's recollection as as pretty a summer room as any country rectory could boast, by being papered .with bright flowery paper all over its sloping roof, and its window made cheerful with climbing plants and flowers; tasteful draperies, a work-table and work-basket in embroidered green satin, book-shelves carved by friends, a piano just good enough for practising upon, and water-colour drawings on the walls.

I have known another room, cheaply fitted up in a French style by a French lady, as a dressing-room, with looking-glass wardrobe and painted furniture. A small bed in an alcove, in case the room might be wanted as a spare room, and lace curtains drawn over the alcove. The head of the bed and all its plain wood-work covered in quilted white cotton in large diamonds, and cross-barred with narrow blue satin ribbon, and large blue bows here and there. The walls papered with a paper resembling quilted muslin. The effect was soft, clean, and extremely pretty.

A few words on the topic of sick-rooms before quitting this part of the subject.

In cases of severe illness it is advisable to engage a professed nurse. She is a great help to the physician, and a support to the family, who too often, in their love for the sufferer, overtax their strength, and break down at the moment this is most required. No person can long sustain night and day nursing, particularly if to bodily fatigue anxiety and distress of mind be added; nor can they keep up that appearance of cheerfulness which is such a support to a sick person. It is a great mistake to attempt to do this in any case, but more especially if it is likely to be a prolonged illness. A sister of mercy is often found a most valuable member of the household under such circumstances. People often talk of not having had their clothes off for a fortnight. One's first thought on hearing this said is, how glad you will be to take a bath! And one's second thought, what good did it do the patient?

The sick-room should be kept as much as possible in its usual order. The paraphernalia of
illness distresses the sick person, causing nervousness. Do not let physic bottles be visible in all
directions, or the patient will never feel well, and
those in attendance will fancy they have caught
the infection, simply because they are nauseated
with the smell of the medicines, and the disagreeable sight of their dregs left about in spoons and
glasses. The medicines that have to be given
at stated hours should be neatly placed in readiness on a small tray, near the clock if possible,
so that they may be remembered and the hours
observed. Keep perfect cleanliness and neatness
in the room, and avoid clatter. Wear thin shoes,
and do not let your dress rustle. A woman's hand
should at every touch improve or replace something, so that there may never be a great bustle
of setting to rights. We have already spoken at
length of ventilation : in sickness it must be particularly attended to, as fresh air is the most
beneficial of all medicines.

At the time of the great cattle-plague, fumiga-

tion with chlorine gas was advocated, and bene-
ficially employed, by Professor Stone, of Owen's
College, Manchester. It is simple for domestic
use.

One teaspoonful of powdered chlorate of potash
should be loosely stirred together with three table-
spoonfuls of dry sand in an empty dry pickle
bottle; add to this nearly an ounce of muriatic
acid ; stand the bottle on some warm embers in
an old Australian-meat tin, or other receptacle of
this kind, and place it (with the embers in it)
on a shelf, or somewhere high up in the room,
taking care not to scorch the wood-work. The
heavy chlorine gas will descend and so fill all
parts of the room, and in about three hours disin-
fection will be complete.

It would be a good thing if district-visitors, and
other charitable persons, would instruct the clergy
and their poor people in such effectual means of
stamping out infection.

In all hospitals "Condy's solution" is placed
with the water and towels for the use of the visiting medical men. It is highly advisable to keep

this in every house for cleansing and disinfecting
purposes, and for the removal of unpleasant smells.
It is useful in cleansing bird-cages and gun-barrels,
in preparing poultry or game, and in many other
ways.

The solution may be made at home. The
British Pharmacopœia allows four grains of the permanganate of potash (the basis of the solution)
to the fluid ounce. It is chiefly for external use.
The permanganate of potash is sold in crystals
of two kinds : the most expensive is the purple,
which is used in what is called the ozonized water,
a very weak solution of permanganate, sold by
chemists for toilet use. The cheaper and more
general disinfectant is a greenish coarse powder,
sold by any honest chemist at under five shillings
a pound.   It may be bought of the General Apo-
thecaries' Company, 49, Berner's Street, London, for
from three shillings a pound to three-and-sixpence,
as it varies with the market; and this does as well
as Condy's patent, and is 500 per cent. cheaper,
as fourteen gallons of disinfectant may be prepared
from a pound of the powdered crystals, and these

again will be extensively diluted for use. The purple crystals may be bought by the ounce.

Be cautious in using this fluid, or the Condy, whichever you may happen to prefer, as it turns almost everything brown that it touches. Very deep stains will never come out ; slight stains wash and wear out after a time, but china and all white ware, and sponges and brushes, have their appearance greatly injured by it. Bed-room floors may be washed with it ; they will be thoroughly purified, and the colour will be as if they were stained dark oak previous to being varnished. Stains will wear off the hands in a few days, and a weak solution will not discolour them. The purple fluid is a test of water—if it turns brown the water is impure. It decolorizes on contact with animal matter.

It is a useful plan to keep a filter on every floor of a house ; the expense is not very great, while the increased safety is incalculable. Spencer's patent, or magnetic-carbide, filter is one of the best. He imitated nature's process when constructing it, having observed that the purest water filtered through oxide of iron in the earth's strata.

Two articles of furniture will be found of great use in a sick-room. One is a chair back with bars of broad webbing, made to lift up and down like the music-desk of a grand piano. This is a most comfortable support to an invalid when sitting up to take food or medicine. When closed flat it will slip easily under the pillow, and it can be raised gently and gradually to the angle required. The other thing is an arm-chair, stood and fastened on a board with four French castors. This is a great assistance in cases of lameness or extreme weakness, as it is easy for the invalid to sit on it and be wheeled to any part of the room ; and it costs less than a wheeled chair.

None of the learned professions have advanced during the last thirty years so much as the medical. Medicine has become a new science since it has taken hold of the sanitary improvement of our towns and dwellings. The profession, with a disinterestedness and devotion to science worthy of liberal minds, combines to make the prevention of disease its aim, even beyond its cure. It forms a noble co-operative society.

At the last meeting of the British Medical Association at Sheffield, it was most truly said that independent medical officers of health would before long change the character of disease throughout the nation, and save future generations much misery. It is to be hoped that the country, which will reap the benefit of their endeavours, will strengthen the hands of those whose efforts are directed to raising the standard of national health.

THE EDUCATION OF GIRLS.

To what age should boys' and girls' education be alike?—Accomplishments fruitlessly taught—Nursery and School-room government—Helplessness—Introduction to society—The convent system—Unhappy results—Scientific education—Geometrical illustration—Religion—Professional life for women—Home training—Varied knowledge—Companionship of a mother—Experience—Kindness—Truth.

AT what age should the training of boys and girls begin to differ? This is a doubtful point, though we may consider that as, until about the age of fourteen, their nature has been much the same, their strength of mind and body nearly equal, and their tastes and dispositions much alike, this may be the time when their training should begin to follow each its own path; as the boy's strength grows from this time beyond that of the girl, while she becomes more remarkable for the increasing delicacy of her skill.

Practically there is a divergence when their clothing begins to differ, but this is merely artificial. The girl is made to wear finer and more delicate clothing than the boy; its texture and form impede her movements, and it is more easily injured by the weather. But where a girl is sensibly dressed, so that her clothes will not spoil with the rain, nor prevent her moving her limbs freely, this diversity between the two disappears.

But although it will not harm a girl to share her brother's pursuits till the age of fourteen, the conditions of her so doing will depend upon circumstances. Except in the case of twins, the boy will be rather older or younger than the girl, if even she have brothers about her own age at all, and many accidents will be found to control her education. Besides these, nature works gradually, and there are seldom abrupt transitions in her processes. The girl's future skill of hand and the boy's strength of arm will be prepared for, and seen, in their differences of taste and choice of pursuits and games; the girl will prefer working for her doll and protecting it from the boy's rough handling, and the boy will love his bat and knife. He will show his instinct for construction, and she hers for preservation, after the first early stage when both alike delight in destruction. Here education comes into use, leading each child to exercise the good instinct instead of its converse.

When the conventional proprieties are not allowed to warp the natural taste, a girl loves running and climbing as well as the boy does: she likes to collect stamps, minerals, fossils, birds' eggs, insects, etc., fully as much as he does. Their favourite books are identical, their scrap-books equally enjoyed, the theatre and theatricals at home delighted in by both, and their pets are much beloved. Why, then, should we make so much difference between them where Nature has created none?

Girls of the upper classes are always at lessons of some kind from six years old to eighteen; thus they have twelve years of instruction, and we know that of old a seven year's apprenticeship was held sufficient to make a master in some craft. What do the twelve years do for our girls? Does their training enable them to maintain them decently in any one line? What have they learnt, and what can they do?

They have learnt music enough to play a *morceau de salon* showily, and the allegretto movement of a sonata stumblingly, and the latter only because it was thought 'proper' that they should learn 'classical music.' But they do not know enough even to learn another *morceau de salon* without the help of a master, so of course music cannot be reckoned upon as doing much for them.

I place music first, because the most time has been given to it; a weary hour every day, had it not been so broken up by visits to the clock. Practical girls grudge this hour wasted on a weakness they are sure to give up when they marry, for they all think they are as certain to marry as to give up their music. They are healthy and strong and have good voices, but few of them can do more than incomprehensibly murmur a few lines of twaddle to a feeble accompaniment, or sing out

of all time the top line of a glee, provided the
piano helps them out with the notes.   So here is a
physical gift thrown aside.

Can anything be made of that pencil-stroking
on buff paper, with some splashes of white, which
is held to represent a cottage, flanked on one side
by a gate-post which could never have been a good
gate-post, and on the other side by something
smeary which is not at all like a tree, nor any other
created thing ?

Every willow-pattern plate has a better landscape on it than that.   So there are two hours
a week gone, for the lop-sided chalk head is of
no more use to anybody than was the landscape.

The girl has been taught French and German,
but has not learnt enough of either language to
enjoy a good book, or to converse with intelligence
in either tongue, and her stock of dialogue-book
phrases is soon exhausted.   Indeed, she can hardly
talk better in English when she gets beyond the
depth of drawing-room chatter, as her knowledge
of facts is of a most uncertain sort ; so in general
conversation she covers her deficiencies by slang,

which, although it distresses us, we forgive in a pretty, lively girl.

She cannot cook, how should she ? She was never permitted to peep inside the kitchen, but was kept in an upstairs nursery until she was six years old, under the stultifying dominion of " nurse," whose sole training was " Miss, I'll tell your ma," when wicked or cruel teaching did not replace this feebleness. When she was promoted to the school-room and made over to the care of the governess, the system of instruction was little more satisfactory. The list of the Kings of England superseded standing in the corner as a punishment for weariness, but her chief experience of life was gathered from tales in cheap magazines, read surreptitiously ; and as she grew older, the railway novel by a sensational author replaced the serial in the penny paper.

The child saw her parents together for a quarter of an hour in the evening, when she was full dressed to go down to dessert, and her mother for about five minutes in the course of the morning, when she came up to the school-room to find

fault with the governess for the children's bad
grammar, or awkward behaviour, on the previous
evening. The round of the year brings the sea-
side visit. Here, although health is gained, there
is no education beyond lodging-house gossip. The
children are put into the train like so many parcels,
and in so many hours are somewhere else; frocks
suited to the sea-side are put on them by the
nurse, but these might have dropped from the
clouds, and the children have been none the wiser.
Helplessness is the natural outcome of all this.

The school-room course begins in about six years
to be agreeably diversified by the visits of music
and drawing-masters; which, if the governess did
not sit in the room all the time, trying to attract
their admiration, would be a really pleasant change.
But nothing comes of the lessons beyond the showy
morceau de salon aforesaid, the buff-paper drawing,
and the weak rhyme jingled to an accompaniment
in quavers; except an increase of energy in borrow-
ing, or hiring, yellow-covered books revealing stirring impossibilities in the lives of Edwin and
Angelina, over which a girl, according to her

disposition, may weep or rage. For this is the only outlet for her poor imprisoned life, until, on her introduction to society, she is suddenly flung upon the world, to make her way as best, or worst, she can ; and now, and now only, does her real education begin.

This manner of bringing up our girls differs from the convent system in this, that it is worldly instead of being religious, and needlework and confectionery are worse taught ; other things are about equal. Both we and our continental neighbours imprison our girls in a school-room or convent for twelve years, and yet boast of our superiority over the Turks !

After this, can we wonder at the weakness or the folly of girls, or be surprised that society is at a dead-lock, or that our women eat bitter bread ?

Can we marvel that women ruin their husbands by their dress and extravagance ; that they drive them to their clubs for companionship, and freedom from the wretchedness of home ; that they tyrannize over their milliners, and are in their turn tyrannized over by their servants ; that their sons drink the brandy and smoke the tobacco of idleness, and that their daughters grow up the patterns of themselves? Only where the mother is passively useless, the daughter will be actively mischievous; where the mother was merely frivolous, the daughter will be actually wicked.

Does all our boasted culture come to this; or will Cambridge examinations and a scientific education set all right again? When an hour a day, at least, for twelve years passed in the study of music has failed to implant those habits of accuracy which this beautiful science so pre-eminently combines with sweetness and grace, is a smattering of geology certain to succeed? Will Greek strengthen the character more than German? Or is one as likely as the other to puff the mind with conceit, where it does not equally encourage a deceitful appearance of knowledge. And is the new system better calculated than the old one to prepare girls for fifty years of womanhood?

People talk of depth, as if truth were only to be found at the bottom of a well. What seems most wanted is breadth, free expansion all round to keep the soul healthy. Let every branch have due encouragement to stretch out towards the light, to receive the shower or sunshine as they come.

Some careful mothers say, "I keep my girls exclusively at 'studies' for the piano; they make such a good groundwork." This may be so, but finger training is not everything. The poor girls have had their souls so sickened over melancholy minor "meditations," that their hearts are closed to the tender or joyous melodies of music, and its rich, majestic harmonies.

Point out these things to the young, who will love them, at first blindly, and afterwards with a gradually developing appreciation.

Here a little, there a little, is a true precept in education. A thing can never be completely taught, for there is infinity everywhere. How rarely we can begin at the beginning, or even the unit, of anything; multiplication and subdivision meet us at both ends, besides all the collaterals.

I have ever observed that those girls who have been the greatest number of years at the same school know the least, and are the most stupid.

It is better to let children go to many different schools in succession, than to remain long in one : they gain more experience, while the chances of their learning evil are the same in both cases. In public schools as boys go up through the forms, they meet different sets of masters and subjects of study, so that these are, in fact, fresh schools.

To use a simile which will be intelligible to this generation, women have been treated as if they were stones. Left shapeless under the school-room prison system, they are only fit to be broken up for the roads, as they will fit in nowhere. Our well-educated ancestresses, down to the time of Hannah More, were formed into cubes, very solid and steady on either of their bases, and suitable for many buildings, though the finer kinds of stone are in this manner misapplied. Modern science gives the stones more sides, and, while seeming to round them into more adaptable forms, only produces a number of small facets, making a somewhat polished dodecahedron, which rolls about in any position and is of no particular service, except, maybe, to stick upon a gate-post at a girl's school,

though it has given a great deal of trouble in the
cutting. But the hourly guidance of the loving
hands of father and mother, aided by raspings and
filings of circumstances, and many blows from
chisels more or less severe, produces at last a beautiful statue, well shaped in all its parts, which
becomes a perfect and nobly planned Galatea.
What is the best training for girls? That is the
question. What are they to be, or not to be?

We have tried hitherto to bring up our girls so
that they may be fitted for the high position here
that we all wish they may attain, making their
education tend solely to pleasure; forgetting how
easily the nature of woman adapts itself to any
superior station, and how soon it seems like everyday life, however high the rank or great the
wealth to which a girl may be suddenly raised.

We teach religion, when it is taught at all, under
the head of "divinity," at school, where it is put
on a par with the multiplication-table; or as a
series of "religious duties," to be performed once
a week and rendered as irksome as possible, quite
ignoring that everything we do is our duty towards

God, or towards our neighbour, which is part of the same duty; whereas we ought to train our girls for "duties" here, and give them joy in preparing for their high position as daughters of God in heaven. We should let our divine life so permeate through every hour of our stay here, that it may be the vivifying light shed upon everything we are concerned with, making the trifles of this life unfold their beauties, comforting sadness and gilding poverty, as the southern sunshine lights up squalid dwellings till they shine like gold and silver, and makes rags glow with light and colour.

Our ideas have changed lately, and now we seem to think that all girls who are not born to high position here must of necessity be trained to professional life. But, after all, the demand for certified teachers, heads of ladies' colleges, doctors, and other learned professions, will never comprise the great bulk of the number of willing workers among the unmarried women of England : nor do these things constitute a quarter of the work to be done.

Instances of marked talent or decided turn for

some particular line of study should be furthered and fostered to the utmost, consistently with the possibility that after all the vocation may not be carried into effect ; but women are really more valuable, and more likely to be happy, in what it is old-fashioned to call the sphere of a home.

And this is best prepared for by home training ; which does not mean being pushed aside so as to be out of the way, and shut up in the nursery or school-room, but enjoying the companionship of a judicious and sensible mother, and the freedom of the house—where the child will be taught to behave herself properly, and be useful and obliging ; where she will have regular hours of study with her mother, her governess, or at school, and yet have opportunities of seeing how everything is managed in the kitchen and throughout the house, being allowed occasionally to do some little thing herself, and so acquire some of the needful practice ; where she can be taught needlework and the proper use of many tools ; learn to carve, to cut bread and butter, to help dishes neatly at table, and gain a knowledge of gardening and green-house culture.

Children should be permitted to look on at the proceedings of all workmen employed in or out of the house : the glazier, gasfitter, gardener, carpet-stretcher, carpenter, locksmith, and piano-tuner ; the exceptions being the dustman and the sweep, because of the dirt.

How much money might be saved in a house if people understood the use of a few tools, the construction of a few fittings, or could take a piano to pieces and tune it. If a bell-wire is broken, a man is sent for ; he charges half a day's work and some materials, and generally makes a little bit of work for some other tradesman, whereas a knowledge of how to unscrew and take off the bell-cover would often enable a piece of copper wire to be joined, and the bell set in order. How often people fail to force down a window whose weights are just over-lapping, where a blow with a mallet on the shutterbox would have shaken them into their places ; or, failing that, the box containing the sash-weights might be opened by taking off the beading near the window-sash, the cords and weights put straight, and the beading replaced by hammering the brads. But no ; we send for a man.

Our water-pipes burst in winter, because during a hard frost we have not taken the precaution to turn the taps so that a few drops may pass to relieve the pressure in thawing.

We cannot even frame and hang up a picture when we have painted it, or cover a chair with the piece of needlework we have made. We do not know how to renew the cord of a spring blind, nor many a little thing besides; and yet any one who keeps a house in order knows how constantly these things are recurring, and what a source of expense they are.

Girls should be taken out shopping that they may learn the names and qualities of things, the quantities of material required for different purposes, and the value of money. The knowledge of how much it costs to clothe a child will teach them more practical arithmetic than any amount of extraction of the square root, and give an interest to their tables of weights and measures besides. Let Euclid be learnt by all means, if desired ; but if it is only done for the sake of training, and not to aid some particular purpose, as good, if not as

exact, training may be found in some study leading to a pleasing result, such as music, drawing, or
knowledge of architecture, as from the pure
mathematics.

Let the girls learn to fit their clothes exactly,
estimate the needful quantity of material, and
calculate the cost of the quality. When the
mother is considering the size and price of a new
carpet, if she consult with her daughters about it, it
will help their judgment at the same time that it
improves their arithmetic. Let girls learn to write
notes of invitation and letters of business, and
write orders to tradespeople ; let them accompany
their parents on house-hunting expeditions—it is
a school in itself—or when furniture is bought.
Elder girls may go with their mothers when they
are treating for schools for little brothers, and when
servants are hired, or evening parties catered for ;
when lodgings are taken for friends, and a thousand
and one other circumstances.

It is all experience, and of the kind those girls
never gain who are always at school-work ; so that
those who have not this knowledge begin life many

years behind the home-trained girls, and commit many follies owing to their want of it. It need not be feared that this experience will destroy a girl's charm of manner. Ignorance is not simplicity, nor silliness a grace, neither are awkwardness and affectation as dignified as self-possession.

I would on no account depreciate the efforts made for the higher education of women. No one rejoices more than I do at seeing things more thoroughly taught. Still, we cannot rest content with crumbs of science; female education must be filled with the milk of human kindness. It is not the nature of woman to stand Alp-like alone, with one peak seeming to pierce the heavens; she should be like the spreading tree which gives shelter and enjoyment to all within its influence, its roots being firmly fixed in the good ground.

The nursery training for children is merely repressive. They are told not to be naughty, not to be greedy, not to break their toys, not to be noisy. Whereas a teaching more calculated to develop their intelligence would substitute some interesting occupation to counteract their naughtiness ; such as mending a toy they have broken, which would delight them more than any new toy ; and having seen the trouble it took to mend it, and the time it took to dry it, they would learn carefulness. If they wish to shout at inconvenient times and places, teach them to sing a chorus, and if the noise is too great, let them sing one at a time. If they are greedy, which often means hungry, for children need frequent feeding, give them a piece of bread.

But although tender kindness is the best of nurture, on no account let it degenerate into weak indulgence. Compel instant obedience to the slightest word, the minutest direction, enforcing habits of attention and discipline. Never let children be obtrusive or feel that they are a power in the house ; and require of them the utmost respect to elders.

The good example of parents is the safeguard of the children. If they show reverence to all that is lovely, children will do so too. Above all, parents should never break a promise, nor ever deceive their children, even in play, or children will not honour their word.

I do not like to see mothers or nurses take away from a child something they do not wish it to have, and hide it, and pretend not to know where it is gone ; yet this is a very favourite form of play, and deemed quite innocent. Surely it were better kindly, but firmly and openly, to remove the object and turn the attention from the loss.

I hope these few remarks will be found useful. I have tried to keep them brief, but in writing on so important a topic as that of education, it is difficult to bear in mind the clever old French saying, "Woe to him who says all that can be said."

SUNDAY.

Children's Sundays made wearisome—Sunday precious to workers
—Moral workers—Moral vices—Our gifts—Misuse of them—
Necessary work on Sunday—Diminished by management—
Sunday prevents us living too fast—The rest must be earned
—Sunday repairs the human machine.

Do not let Sunday be turned into a day of dread
to the children. It is the day which the Lord has
made; we will rejoice and be glad in it. For years
I lived in terror of the Sunday, and I feel for
children who, being brought more into the presence
of their elders on that day, are consequently more
exposed to reproof for their natural animal spirits,
which are trying to jaded and irritable persons.
An only child, I was taken twice a day to a church
built in the dismal style of the reign of George III.,
and put into a high pew, "shut up in a cupboard,"

as I have heard a little child express it, where I could only see a frightful ornament like a row of teeth in painted woodwork that ran round the upper part of the church. I sat contemplating this through the long low church service and sermon, of which I was too young to understand a word. The remainder of the day was filled up with collect, epistle, and catechism, Bible questions to write and answer, the text to remember, hymns to repeat to visitors, and a prolonged dessert, with half a glass of sherry, which was like a dose of physic to me. The " Life of Joseph " was my only recreation.

Too often is Sunday given up to the display of toilet vanities out of doors and listlessness at home. Those who have been really working during the week know well what a blessing the Sunday rest is. Those who have been idle cannot expect to feel this, and they experience such a flatness in the quietly kept Sunday that they regard it as a weekly penance which interrupts their pleasures. But they ought not to have allowed themselves to get into this condition of feeling. There is work for all in the world ; none but the dead have a right to be idle.

As Kingsley justly asks : " If vanity, profligacy, pride, and idleness be not moral vices, what are ? " What is more common than to find pride and vanity leading our women to idleness, and that extravagance and craving after gaiety which are the feminine form of profligacy ? And Kingsley goes on to show that beneath these vices, and perhaps the cause of them all, lies another and deeper vice—godlessness, atheism.

" I do not," continues he, " mean merely the want of religion, doctrinal unbelief. I mean want of belief in duty, in responsibility. Want of belief that there is a living God governing the universe, who has set us our work, and will judge us according to our work."

Why are our noble gifts given to us ; such gifts as these—

> " The reason firm, the temperate will,
> Endurance, foresight, strength, and skill."

Is it that we may become " tolerably harmless dolls ? " How shall we answer for having used our endurance only so much as may make us wait with common patience for next month's number of *Belgravia;* our foresight in choosing a pattern for a mantle which shall be fashionable enough to be worn next autumn; our skill in crochet-work, and our strength in skating on the outside edge.

No wonder we do not value the Sunday rest. We know that heavenly mansions are being prepared for us to enjoy the heavenly rest in, and that we must prepare ourselves for these mansions, or we shall not be permitted to enter them. Then let us take pains to prepare our earthly houses for the right use of the day of rest, and be able to go up to the house of the Lord with the multitude that keep holy-day.

We should so put our houses in order on Saturday that we may really be able to rest on Sunday. Some works of necessity must be done, such as the dinner prepared; but by dining early, and doing as much as possible on the previous day towards its preparation, the labour may be reduced to a minimum.

There will be no needlework, no cleaning or

dusting, no marketing to be done on Sunday. Pies and tarts should have been made on Saturday, a double quantity of potatoes and other vegetables prepared, and a general foresight used.

Sunday is a good day for sending out a large joint to be baked, and a pudding also; indeed, this seems the opportunity for the national roast beef and plumpudding dinner. So that, in fact, beyond laying the cloth and removing the things used at meals, there is absolutely no work to be done beyond the five minutes' daily occupation of each person in making his or her own bed, as the re-arrangement of the used dinner things may be left till the following morning. The table is cleared as if by magic, if every child is told to put in its place two things, or three things, according to the number of things used and the number of children to put them back. Each person replaces his or her own chair, and the Sunday work is over. Life is not so hard to us as it was to the country squire's wife half a century ago, who always gave her servants physic on a Sunday because it was no loss of time. To us the Sunday is very helpful in another way: it keeps us from living too fast; without this wholesome stop we might drive ourselves on to frenzy.

Many if not most of us feel lazy and desultory on Monday morning (which therefore had better be employed on some kind of desultory and irregular work), and we only get ourselves warm in the harness by the middle of the week. We go on working with gradually increasing excitement until Saturday night, when some sensible friend hints that it is too late to make a bad week's work good; precious Sunday comes to ease the strain, and the human machine is oiled and cooled.

Let us be diligent during the week, and lengthen our days by beginning them earlier, so as to do most of our work in the morning; then with a clear conscience we may leave off our play as early as we please and go to rest: we shall enjoy the Sunday repose which we have earned, and find ourselves refreshed instead of wearied by it.

I will conclude this essay in the words of Macaulay—words which he considers among the very best he ever wrote. "Man, man is the great instrument that produces wealth. The natural difference between Campania and Spitzbergen is trifling when compared with the difference between a country inhabited by men full of bodily and mental vigour, and a country inhabited by men sunk in bodily and mental decrepitude. Therefore it is that we are not poorer but richer, because we have, through many ages, rested from our labour one day in seven. That day is not lost. While industry is suspended, while the plough lies in the furrow, while the Exchange is silent, while no smoke ascends from the factory, a process is going on quite as important to the wealth of nations as any process which is performed on more busy days. Man, the machine of machines, the machine compared with which all the contrivances of the Watts and Arkwrights are worthless, is repairing and winding up, so that he returns to his labours on the Monday with clearer intellect, with livelier spirits, with renewed corporal vigour. Never will I believe that what makes a population stronger and healthier and wiser and better can ultimately make it poorer.

" If ever we are forced to yield the foremost place among commercial nations, we shall yield it not to a race of degenerate dwarfs, but to some people pre-eminently vigorous in body and in mind."

THE END.

PRINTED AT THE CAXTON PRESS, BECCLES.